Kathy's Baby-sitting Hassle

Other Crossway Books by
Hilda Stahl

THE SADIE ROSE ADVENTURE SERIES
Sadie Rose and the Daring Escape
Sadie Rose and the Cottonwood Creek Orphan
Sadie Rose and the Outlaw Rustlers
Sadie Rose and the Double Secret
Sadie Rose and the Mad Fortune Hunters
Sadie Rose and the Phantom Warrior
Sadie Rose and the Champion Sharpshooter
Sadie Rose and the Secret Romance
(more to follow)

GROWING UP ADVENTURES
Sendi Lee Mason and the Milk Carton Kids
Sendi Lee Mason and the Stray Striped Cat
Sendi Lee Mason and Big Mistake
Sendi Lee Mason and the Great Crusade

KAYLA O'BRIAN ADVENTURES
Kayla O'Brian and the Dangerous Journey
Kayla O'Brian: Trouble at Bitter Creek Ranch
Kayla O'Brian and the Runaway Orphans
(more to follow)

DAISY PUNKIN
Meet Daisy Punkin
The Bratty Brother
(more to follow)

BEST FRIENDS
#1: Chelsea and the Outrageous Phone Bill
#2: Big Trouble for Roxie
#4: Hannah and the Special 4th of July
(more to follow)

Best Friends

#3

Kathy's Baby-sitting Hassle

Hilda Stahl

CROSSWAY BOOKS • WHEATON, ILLINOIS
A DIVISION OF GOOD NEWS PUBLISHERS

Kathy's Baby-sitting Hassle.

Published by Crossway Books, a division of
Good News Publishers, 1300 Crescent Street, Wheaton, Illinois 60187.

Cover illustration: Paul Casale

First printing, 1992

Printed in the United States of America

Library of Congress Cataloging-in-Publication Data

Stahl, Hilda.
Kathy's baby-sitting hassle / Hilda Stahl.
p. cm. — (Best friends : #3)
Summary: As caring for her little sister becomes more disagreeable, Kathy turns to God for help.
[1. Sisters—Fiction. 2. Christian Life—Fiction.] I. Title.
II. Series: Stahl, Hilda. Best friends : #3.
PZ7.S78244Kat 1992 91-43088
ISBN 0-89107-659-X

---

00 99 98
15 14 13 12 11 10 9 8 7 6

Dedicated with love to
Felicia

Contents

1	Missing!	9
2	Betina Quinn	19
3	*King's Kids* Meeting	29
4	Strange Happenings	43
5	The Visit	51
6	The New Job	59
7	Duke	67
8	Help	79
9	Lee Malcomb	89
10	Natalie	101
11	The Picnic	115
12	Unsettled	125
13	Mark and Allie	135
14	More Trouble	143
15	A Talk with Dad	151

1

Missing!

Sighing impatiently, Kathy stood in the grass at the entrance of the park with her little sister Megan. Children ran and played, shouting and laughing in the bright morning sunshine. A few adults sat on benches in the shade of the giant maples and oaks. Kathy frowned down at Megan. "I brought you to the park, but that doesn't mean I have to play with you!"

Megan puckered up, ready to cry. "Why don't you like me, Kathy?"

Kathy's heart lurched, and she flushed with guilt. "I do like you, Megan! I love you! But you're four and I'm eleven. I don't always want to play with you. And you don't always want to play with me."

"Yes, I do."

Kathy looked off across the park while she struggled to hold back her anger. She hated baby-sitting Megan! It just wasn't fair. Duke was twelve, a year older than she, and he *never* had to watch Megan.

"I'm too hot," Megan said as she tugged at her sweater.

"Mom told you to leave it on until it got really warm," Kathy said, closing the sweater over Megan's pink blouse. She fixed the wide pink bands around Megan's ponytails and brushed dirt from the sandbox off her jeans.

"I want to swing," Megan said, tugging on the bottom of Kathy's T-shirt.

Kathy forced back a sharp answer. "Then go swing," she said as kindly as she could.

"Will you push me?" Megan looked up at Kathy with wide brown eyes just like Mom's.

Kathy shrugged. She sure didn't have anything better to do right now. "All right . . . For a while." She impatiently brushed back her blonde curls from her flushed cheeks. She and Duke were blonde and blue-eyed like Dad. Sometimes it embarrassed her because Dad's hair was longer than hers, and he wore it in a ponytail. Her hair was naturally curly, and when it got too long she couldn't get even a hair pick with four-inch teeth through it.

Megan ran to the swings for kids her age. She struggled to get on the orange plastic seat. She clung tightly to the chains, the tips of her sneakers barely touching the bare spot in the grass under the swing.

Sighing with boredom, Kathy pushed Megan back and forth on the swing. The chains creaked, and Megan giggled. Just as Kathy was ready to tell Megan to swing by herself she saw her best friends—Chelsea, Roxie, and Hannah—walk into the park. Now she had somebody to talk to! "You keep swinging, Megan. I want to talk to the girls."

Megan sighed. "All right. I'll talk to Natalie."

Kathy spun around and frowned at Megan. Natalie was Megan's make-believe friend, but she'd given her up just last month, much to the family's relief. "You can talk to me, Megan. I won't be long."

Megan smiled as she swung back and forth. "I want to talk with Natalie. She has a good secret she wants to tell me."

Kathy hesitated. "Not Natalie. If you wait *I'll* tell you a secret." She didn't want to leave Megan, but she needed to talk to her friends. "I'll be right back. Okay, Megan?"

"Sure," said Megan. She looked at the swing beside her. "Okay, Natalie?" She nodded and looked back at Kathy. "Natalie said you can take all the time you want."

Kathy groaned. Was it her fault Megan had brought Natalie back? Kathy ran to meet Chelsea, Hannah, and Roxie. They all wore buttons on their T-shirts that said *I'm A Best Friend*. Kathy touched her shirt. She'd left her button on her dresser! "Hi," she said as they met near the wishing well. Maybe they wouldn't notice she had forgotten her button. She, Roxie, and Hannah had gotten them three days ago to match Chelsea's and had promised to wear them all the time.

Her blue eyes sparkling, Chelsea flipped back her long red ponytail and said in her Oklahoma accent, "We have the most exciting news to tell you about *King's Kids*!" *King's Kids* were kids who did odd jobs for pay (plus occasional good deeds for free). Chelsea's mom had thought of the name for the business. She'd said, "Jesus is the King, and you are His kids." Their motto was, "Great or small, we do it all."

"What's the news?" asked Kathy as she glanced at the others. Her pulse leaped just looking at them. All three were ready to burst. Chelsea, the president of *King's Kids*, was the only one of the four that hadn't been born and raised right in Middle Lake, Michigan. Hannah, the treasurer, was a Native American, and her family had lived in Michigan since even before the giant white pines were lumbered in the 1800s. Roxie, the secretary, lived next door to Chelsea and across the street from Hannah. They all three lived in a subdivision called The Ravines, just across the street from her house on Kennedy Street.

"We have a job for all four of us that will last the rest of the summer!" Roxie twirled around. Her cap of dark hair bounced, and her dark eyes snapped.

"All summer," whispered Hannah in awe as she pushed her long dark hair back over her shoulder.

"What is it?" asked Kathy, barely able to stand still.

All three girls started telling Kathy the details. She laughed and held out her hand. "I can't understand a word you're saying." They stopped talking and giggled.

"I'll tell it," said Roxie, sounding very important. "I *am* the secretary." She took a deep breath. "Paul and Sonya Crandall are going away for the whole summer. They live on our street at The Ravines. They want us to . . ." Roxie began to count with her fingers. ". . . keep their house clean, plants watered, pets tended, garden weeded, lawn mowed, and their mail and newspapers taken inside."

"They have two cats, two dogs, and some fish," said Chelsea.

"It's a major job," said Roxie.

"Every single day!" cried Hannah and Chelsea.

"And they'll pay a lot of money," Roxie said with a squeal.

Kathy gasped. It sounded too good to be true. "When do we start?"

"Tomorrow," said Chelsea. *She* was especially excited about it because she desperately needed money to pay off her huge phone bill. After her family had moved from Oklahoma, she'd called her best friend every day and talked to her a long time. Her parents said she had to pay the bill because it was her responsibility to accept the consequences of her actions. She'd started *King's Kids* for that very reason.

Kathy sighed heavily. "What about me? I have to watch Megan every Tuesday all day long and some afternoons."

"We'll work around your schedule," said Chelsea.

"Where is Megan?" asked Hannah.

"On the swing," said Kathy.

"No, she's not," Hannah said.

Kathy spun around. Her heart zoomed to her feet. Megan's sweater lay in a heap on the ground under the swing, but she wasn't there! "Where is she?" Kathy screamed, looking frantically around as she ran here and there. "Where is she?"

"She has to be here someplace," said Roxie, sounding almost as frightened as Kathy.

"I should've stayed right with her!" Kathy burst into tears.

"We'll find her," Hannah said, patting Kathy's arm.

"We'll all look for her," Chelsea said.

"It'll be my fault if anything happens to her!" wailed Kathy, wringing her hands.

Hannah caught Kathy's hands and held them tightly. "Shhh. Calm down. God is with us, and He'll help us find her."

"That's right . . . That's right," Kathy said, brushing frantically at her tears. Her heart pounded so hard, she thought it would break right through her skin.

"We'll each take a section of the park," Chelsea said. "Then we'll all come back to the swings in five minutes."

Kathy twisted Megan's sweater around and around her hand as she ran toward the sandbox. "Jesus, forgive me for leaving Megan alone," Kathy whispered hoarsely. Maybe Megan was hiding behind the bushes near the sandbox. She looked there, but no Megan. She asked the kids nearby, but they hadn't noticed Megan. Kathy looked behind the bushes near the wishing well too. "Keep her safe, Jesus." She glanced at her watch. Time was up. Blood pounding in her ears, she raced back to the swings the same time as her friends did.

"Now where shall we look?" asked Roxie.

Kathy couldn't speak around the hard lump in her throat. Oh, why hadn't she stayed with Megan! Mom and Dad had warned her over and over and over never to leave Megan alone. If she found Megan, she'd never leave her alone again as long as she lived! Silently she prayed again that God would keep Megan safe and that they'd find her soon.

"Let's all stay together and look for her," Chelsea said.

Hannah looked around thoughtfully. "We know she didn't run by us while we were talking. She probably went that way." Hannah pointed off toward the wooded area at the edge of the park.

Kathy hung on every word Hannah spoke. Kathy knew Hannah liked solving mysteries. She liked sorting out details and making deductions.

Hannah nodded and said, "I say we see if she went in those woods."

Roxie gasped. "I heard there's a mean woman who lives in a huge house in there."

Kathy trembled. What if the mean woman had caught Megan and was doing something really bad to her?

"Let's get going," Chelsea said impatiently. "We can't find her just standing here."

Fear stung Kathy's fingertips as she ran to the trees with the girls. They found a narrow path through the woods, and they followed it, knowing Megan would do that rather than fight her way through underbrush—if she had come this way at all.

Suddenly the trees ended at a wide lawn that led to a huge, white three-story house. The lawn needed mowing. Weeds grew as tall as the flowers in the flower beds. Birds sang in the trees. A cottontail rabbit hopped from the base of an empty birdbath to the edge of a flower bed.

"I don't think anyone lives here," Chelsea whispered as she stepped closer to Hannah.

"We have to look," Kathy said. Her mouth was bone-dry, and her tongue felt twice as big as normal.

Staying close together, they walked to the back door and listened. A slight noise came from the side of the house. They crept around the house to a porch that ran from one end of the house to the other. It had a white railing with white spindles. Megan was sitting on a white wooden porch swing with a woman none of them knew. Megan was telling the woman about her make-believe friend Natalie. The woman was about Kathy's mom's age. She had long brown hair that needed brushing. She wore a gray T-shirt much too large on her slender body and faded jeans. Kathy bit her lip to hold back a cry.

"It's the mean woman," whispered Roxie.

Kathy's legs almost collapsed under her. She gripped Chelsea for support.

"Stay calm," Hannah whispered.

Kathy clung tightly to Chelsea's arm as she walked toward the wide steps that led up to the porch.

2

Betina Quinn

Kathy stopped on the bottom step with Chelsea, Roxie, and Hannah close behind her. "Megan," Kathy said softly.

Megan looked up and smiled. "Hi, Kathy. Me and Natalie and Betina have been talking."

The woman jumped up, her face full of fear. "What do you girls want?" she asked hoarsely. Her gray T-shirt hung almost to her knees. Her tangled hair looked as if she hadn't washed it in days.

Megan slipped off the swing and took the woman's hand. "Don't be scared, Betina. That's my sister Kathy and her friends. I told you about them."

Betina studied the girls, then glanced wildly at the French door just beyond them. "I don't want you here! Leave right now!"

"We only came for Megan," Hannah said softly as she slowly walked up the steps. She put her hand out. "Come on, Megan."

Betina caught Megan's arm. "She can't go with you."

Kathy gasped, and all the color drained from her face. "I have to take her home," Kathy whispered. "Tell her, Megan."

Smiling up at Betina, Megan said, "I have to go with my sister. I'll come another day to see you."

"I want you to stay," Betina said with a catch in her voice.

Kathy held her breath. Would Betina grab Megan and run into the house so they couldn't get her back? She felt the others stiffen.

"I like you, Betina," said Megan, "but I can't stay." She turned to Kathy. "Can I?"

"No," Kathy said hoarsely. "It's almost time for lunch and your nap."

"I'll give you lunch," Betina said, stroking Megan's hair. "You can take a nap here. I have lots of beds."

Kathy finally found the strength to step closer to Betina. "We can all come see you again. Right now we have to go home. Would you like us all to come again?"

Betina chewed on her bottom lip as she continued to stroke Megan's soft hair. "I want Megan to stay."

Megan touched Betina's hand. "I'll leave Natalie with you, so you won't be lonely. Want me to?"

Betina's eyes filled with tears. "But she's your very best friend."

Kathy's stomach knotted. How could an adult feel about Natalie like Megan did?

"I know," said Megan, smiling. "But Natalie likes you as much as I do, and she thinks it would be fun to stay here with you. She likes your big house. She wants to see all your beds."

Kathy didn't dare look at her friends. She hadn't told them about Natalie. They might think Megan was crazy.

Betina bent down and kissed Megan's cheek. "Leave Natalie then. I'll see you another day." Betina straightened and looked sharply at Kathy. "Do you promise to bring Megan back again?"

Kathy's heart sank. If she promised, she'd have to keep her word. "I'll try to bring her back. I have to ask my dad."

"She'll bring me back," said Megan. "I have to get Natalie, you know."

"That's right." Betina smiled, taking some of the strain out of her face. "I'll see you tomorrow." She turned to the girls. "You girls can come too, if you want."

"Thank you," said Kathy stiffly. Would Mom and Dad let them come back? She held her hand out to Megan. "We have to go now, Megan."

"Okay," Megan said cheerily. She took Kathy's hand, then looked back at Betina. "Bye for now.

Bye, Natalie. Be a good girl, and don't talk too much."

Kathy wanted to fall through the steps out of sight. Megan's words were a very echo of her own. She was always telling Megan not to talk so much.

Betina sat back on the swing. "We'll swing, Natalie, then I'll take you in for your nap."

Gripping Megan's hand, Kathy hurried as fast as she could back to the path. Chelsea, Hannah, and Roxie followed. Nobody spoke until they were in the park again. The girls dropped to the grass. Kathy pulled Megan down beside her. It seemed strange to hear shouts and laughter from the kids playing behind them.

"I was so scared!" whispered Roxie.

"Me too," said Kathy and Chelsea.

"How come?" asked Megan.

"She didn't seem mean," said Hannah.

"I felt sorry for her," said Chelsea. "Once in Oklahoma I knew a woman who acted strange like that. It was because she never had anybody around to talk to."

"I don't know if I dare tell Mom and Dad about this," Kathy said, holding Megan's sweater tight against her chest. She sighed heavily. "But I know I have to."

"I hope you don't get in too much trouble," murmured Chelsea.

"I don't know if we should go back," said Roxie, shivering.

"I think we should," announced Hannah.

"I'm hungry!" Megan jumped up. "You said we were going to eat."

"We are." Kathy stood up, her legs still a little unsteady. "I'll see you girls later." They had a *King's Kids* meeting at Chelsea's house at 4.

"Later," said the girls.

Several minutes later Kathy hesitated outside their kitchen door, then followed Megan in. Dad was already making cheese sandwiches. He looked up with a grin.

"Hi. I was beginning to think you girls forgot the time," he said. His ponytail swished across his thin back as he reached into the refrigerator for a gallon of milk.

"Sorry we're late," Kathy answered.

"I made a new friend," Megan said as she climbed on a stool at the island counter. "Her name is Betina Quinn. We talked and laughed. I left Natalie with her."

Kathy held her breath as Dad shot her a questioning look. Dad felt bad about Megan's having a make-believe friend. He thought it was his fault for not being able to spend more time with her.

"We're going to visit Betina again," Megan said as she picked up a tiny piece of cheese and stuck it in her mouth.

Dad gave Kathy a look that said, "I want to hear all about this later when Megan's in bed." Aloud he said, "Betina Quinn . . . I've heard that name before."

"She lives in that huge house near the park," Kathy said, leaning against the counter to keep from falling. She wondered if she'd ever get over the scare of losing Megan.

"She has a swing on her porch," said Megan.

"Yes! The Quinn estate!" Dad whistled and shook his head. "She's one rich lady . . . A real recluse."

"What does that mean?" asked Kathy.

"She won't see or talk to anyone. I heard she even sent her housekeeper and gardener away."

"She talked to me and Natalie," said Megan.

"What's wrong with her?" asked Kathy.

Dad set the sandwiches on the table and filled the glasses on the counter with milk. "A few months ago her husband and little girl were killed in a car wreck. She locked herself away and won't let anyone help her in her grief."

"That's sad," Kathy said as she set the glasses on the table. She finally felt her strength return.

"Did she want you to visit again?" asked Dad.

"We have to," said Megan. "Natalie's there."

Kathy flushed at Megan's words, but answered Dad. "Yes. She said to come visit tomorrow. She even invited Chelsea, Roxie, and Hannah."

"Then I think you should go," said Dad with a nod. "You could be a big help to her. I know a friend of hers . . . Lee Malcomb. He's been praying for her since the accident. She won't let him near her or the estate."

Megan yawned and rubbed her eyes.

"Let's eat," said Dad. "It looks like one little girl is ready for a nap."

"Not me," said Megan. "I'm not tired."

Later, after Megan was asleep, Dad called Kathy into his music room. Her legs felt full of concrete as she walked past his piano to the leather couch that stood to the left of the row of windows and the French doors. A guitar and a bass stood side by side on stands near a keyboard and a sound system.

"I don't have another student for a few minutes," Dad said as he perched on his stool, his heels locked on the bottom rung of the stool, his hands resting on his bony knees. His blue eyes seemed to pierce right through Kathy. "Now suppose you tell me exactly what happened today."

Kathy sat on her icy hands and looked down at the rust-colored carpet. How she wished she could lie! But she knew she couldn't. Jesus didn't want her to. Slowly she told Dad the whole story.

Dad was quiet a long time. "I know I'm supposed to know how to deal with this since I'm the parent, but I don't . . . I don't know what to say."

Kathy's eyes filled with tears. "I'm sorry, Dad. I know it was wrong for me to leave Megan alone. I know something really, really bad could've happened to her." A tear slipped down Kathy's cheek. "And I know it's my fault Natalie is back. I am so sorry!"

Dad sat on the couch and pulled Kathy close. She smelled his aftershave and felt the thud of his heart.

"Honey, I know you're sorry. So am I. Especially about Natalie." Dad wiped Kathy's face with a tissue, then grinned at her. "God is with us, Kit Kat."

"I sure prayed when we couldn't find Megan."

"And you found her. Praise God!" Dad walked back to his stool and sat on it again. "I'm glad you've learned the importance of keeping your eye on Megan." He rubbed his hand over his eyes. "What a hard way to learn!" He cleared his throat. "You girls can visit Betina again. I hope you can help her over her grief."

"I hope so too." Kathy didn't know what they could do, but they'd try to be friends with her if she'd let them.

Dad glanced at his watch. "Time for you to run along now. My student will be here any minute." He rolled his eyes. "He doesn't know an E from a C. And he's been taking piano for two months already!"

Kathy laughed as she walked toward the door that led into the hall. She knew how tired Dad got of students who wouldn't practice or learn the notes.

"Oh, I forgot to tell you."

Kathy turned and waited.

"Brooke Sobol and her sister Pearl went to see Brooke's daughter Penny and her family. They'll be gone two weeks. She asked if you'd keep your eye on the place."

Kathy shrugged. "Sure." She was glad Mrs. Sobol was finally going to get to meet the grandchildren she'd never seen.

"She'll pay you when she returns."

"Okay."

Dad winked. "If she remembers she even said that."

Kathy giggled. "Her memory is a lot better now that her daughter Penny has come back and she's not fighting with Pearl."

"Anyway, she left the key in the same place."

Kathy nodded, said good-bye, and walked out just as Dad's student walked through the French doors. Kathy stopped at the window that looked out on Mrs. Sobol's yard and house. The yard was neatly mowed. She'd watch it for Mrs. Sobol as a favor, not for pay. It would be her good deed. The *King's Kids* all agreed to do three good deeds a week. This would be one, and visiting Betina Quinn would be another.

Kathy smiled as she walked to her room to finish the book she'd started yesterday.

3

King's Kids Meeting

Kathy sat cross-legged on the floor in Chelsea's mauve and blue bedroom and listened as Roxie read the minutes to last week's meeting. It didn't take long to read them even though they filled four pages of Roxie's notebook. She wrote big.

"That's all," said Roxie, flipping the book closed.

"Now, Kathy, you can tell us everything!" said Chelsea.

"Was your dad mad?" asked Hannah.

"Did you get grounded?" wondered Roxie.

Kathy took a deep breath and told them *everything*. It felt good to know she didn't have to keep any secrets from them. She even told them about Natalie, and they didn't think Megan was crazy or anything.

"I want to go with you tomorrow," Hannah said. "I want to see Betina smile."

"I want to see her house." Roxie rolled her eyes. "I bet it's better than the nice houses we see on TV."

"It probably has a million bedrooms," Hannah added dreamily. "And I don't even have one! I still think I should make a bedroom in our basement."

"You'd be able to sleep all night without hearing your new baby brother," said Chelsea, laughing.

"I wonder if they have a sauna and a hot tub and all that stuff," asked Roxie.

"I think we should give Betina our ad," Chelsea said excitedly. "She might want to hire the *King's Kids*! I might be able to make enough to pay off my entire phone bill!"

"We'll go tomorrow afternoon after Megan wakes up from her nap." Kathy grinned sheepishly. "That's when I have to watch her, so why not do both things at once?"

Just then the phone rang, and Chelsea quickly answered it. She listened for a while as she scribbled on the pad beside the phone. "I'll call you later to let you know if we can do the job, Mr. Teski." Chelsea hung up and turned to the others. "Do any of you know Eli Teski on Pine Street, outside The Ravines?"

"No," Kathy said at the same time Hannah and Roxie did. They never went to work for anyone unless they knew him or her or checked him or her out thoroughly.

Frowning thoughtfully, Roxie tapped her pencil on her notebook. "Who would know someone over on Pine?"

"Nick might," Chelsea said, flushing. She liked Nick and was always trying to find a way to talk to him.

"He might," Roxie said. "Give him a call."

Kathy giggled when Chelsea grabbed the phone before Roxie had the words out of her mouth. Kathy had liked Pete Newberry last year, but he moved away, and she didn't like any special boy now. It was fun to watch Chelsea and Nick together.

Chelsea talked only a few minutes. She looked grim when she hung up.

Kathy's stomach tightened. "What?" she asked sharply.

"Nick says not to have anything to do with Eli Teski. He's been to jail for molesting kids." Chelsea trembled. "I don't even want to call him back!"

"I will!" said Roxie gruffly. She scooped up the phone, and when Eli Teski answered she said, "This is Roxie from the *King's Kids*. We can't work for you now or ever." She hung up with a bang. "There!"

Kathy pressed her hands to her ashen cheeks. "What if we hadn't checked on him?"

Chelsea jumped up and looked down at the girls. "I promised my mom and dad that we'd never

ever work for someone without checking on them. We will never break that rule!"

"Never!" the others cried.

With a sigh Chelsea sat back down on the floor and leaned against her bed. "Sometimes I get really scared about . . . about . . . things like that," she whispered.

Kathy nodded as Roxie and Hannah agreed. Kathy took a deep breath. "We have angels watching over us to protect us," she said softly. "We have to be careful, but we don't have to be afraid—that's what my dad says."

"That's right," Hannah said with a nod.

Roxie wrapped her arms around her knees and leaned forward. "Sometimes I think about all the murders and stuff and I'm almost too scared to leave my house."

Kathy reached in her pocket and pulled out a scrap of paper. The Best Friends had agreed to take turns finding a special Bible verse for each day for all of them. Today was her day. "Let me read my verse. It's good for this very minute." She felt their eyes on her as she read, "'God has not given us the spirit of fear, but of power and love and a sound mind.' 2 Timothy 1:7." She took a deep breath. "It means if we're ever fearful, it's not God making us afraid . . . it's the devil. He wants us to be scared and afraid to do anything, even walk out our doors. God has given us power and love and a sound mind. So when we're afraid we just have to say, 'No! Fear doesn't belong to me! I will not fear! I am full of power and love from God and I have a sound mind.'"

Hannah nodded. "That's right."

"That's a good verse," said Roxie. She didn't know as much about the Bible as the others. "I want to write that down so I can remember it." She flipped open her notebook and scribbled the verse on a blank page. She used most of the page for it.

Just then the phone rang again, and they all jumped, then giggled.

On the third ring Chelsea had herself in control enough to answer. She listened, then answered, "Yes. She's right here." She held the phone out to Kathy. "It's your dad."

In surprise Kathy took it and said, "Hello."

"Hi, Kit Kat. I'm sorry to bother you in your meeting, but I need you to come take care of Megan. Mom will be home in about an hour, but I have to leave now."

"What about Duke?"

"He's not here either. Sorry."

Kathy bit back a sigh. "I'll be right home."

"Thanks, Kathy. You're a real helper."

Kathy slowly hung up. "I have to watch Megan. Again! Oh, I get so tired of it!" She clamped her hand over her mouth, and her eyes filled with tears. How could she say that after what had happened this morning?

"I get tired of watching Faye," Roxie said with a nod. "Little sisters aren't always fun."

Hannah nodded. "I have *three* little sisters . . . and a baby brother! I know what you both mean!"

"I have a little brother and he's as bad as a little sister," said Chelsea.

Kathy brushed away her tears. "I thought you'd think I was awful."

"We don't," they all said at once.

Kathy jumped up. "I gotta go. See you all later."

"Bye."

Kathy ran downstairs and outdoors to her bike. She pedaled home as fast as she could. There was something in Dad's voice that was different. Was something wrong?

She ran through the back door and called, "I'm home, Dad."

He dashed from the bathroom, kissed her cheek, and said, "Megan's watching *Cinderella*. See you in a couple of hours."

Frowning, Kathy watched him run to his car and drive away. What was going on? She walked slowly to the living room. Megan was sitting on the floor with her eyes glued to the TV. She'd watched that video a hundred times, but she never got tired of it.

Kathy sat in the corner of the couch and watched. She wanted to get her book from her bedroom, but she got caught up in the story.

When the movie ended Megan shut it off and pushed the rewind button. The whirr seemed loud in the quiet room. "I wish I was Cinderella," Megan said as she crawled onto Kathy's lap. "I want friends like hers and a dress and everything."

The back door banged. Megan jumped up with a shout. "Mom's home!"

Kathy followed Megan to the back door. Mom taught school during the year, but in the summers she tutored kids who needed extra help. She looked tired as she dropped her bundle of things on the island. She was short and somewhat overweight. She wore a cool cotton dress and tan sandals.

"Where's your dad?" she asked as she sank to a chair and fanned herself with her hand.

"I don't know," Kathy said, filling a glass with iced tea from the refrigerator. She handed it to Mom as she told about Dad calling her home.

"Thanks, Kit Kat!" Mom drank half of it, then sighed heavily. "I am tired!" She smiled at Kathy and Megan as they sat at the table with her. "How was your day?"

Kathy shrugged. She didn't want to tell Mom what had happened.

Megan sat on her knees on the chair and leaned her elbows on the table. Her dark eyes that were just like Mom's sparkled. "I left Natalie with my new friend Betina."

Mom's hand tightened around her glass. She darted a look at Kathy, then said to Megan, "Where'd you meet your new friend?"

"At her house," said Megan. "We were at the park, and Natalie and me wanted to go for a walk. So we did, and we found Betina."

Kathy's stomach fluttered. She hated to have to tell Mom what she'd done, but she took a deep breath and told her. "Dad said we should go again tomorrow."

"I have to get Natalie," Megan said, nodding.

"Why don't you leave Natalie with Betina?" asked Mom with a stiff smile.

"I can't." Megan pushed back her ponytails and looked very wise. "She still has a secret to tell me. We share secrets because we're best friends."

Kathy sank low in her chair. She'd told Megan that very thing about Chelsea, Roxie, and Hannah.

They talked a while longer, and then Mom said she wanted to change into shorts and a cool blouse. Megan went with her, but Kathy just sagged in her chair.

"Something wrong, Kit Kat?"

Kathy glanced up at the sound of Dad's voice. Then she leaped up, her eyes round and her mouth hanging open. Dad no longer had a ponytail! His hair was short and waved back off his forehead and over his ears! He wore black dress pants and a white shirt! "Dad?" She slowly walked all around him. Never in a million years would she have recognized him.

He laughed. "Am I that much of a shock?"

In all her eleven years she'd never seen him with short hair and clothes like other dads wore. "Why did you do it?"

"Don't you like the change?"

"Yes! But, Dad . . . I don't know if it's really you!"

He laughed and hugged her tight. She smelled his aftershave and felt his heart thud against her. It *was* Dad!

"I'll explain the change when we're all together. Where's Mom?"

"Changing. Megan's with her. Duke's not home yet." Kathy sank down on her chair and stared at Dad. He was tall and lean and good-looking.

Just then Mom walked in with Megan chattering at her side. They stopped short. Mom clamped her hand over her mouth, and Megan suddenly turned shy.

"Tommy?" whispered Mom.

"It's me all right, Grace." Dad grinned as he turned to give her an all-around view.

Mom tipped back her head and laughed like Kathy had never heard her laugh before.

"Are you really my dad?" asked Megan suspiciously, hanging back against Mom.

"Sure am," said Dad.

"Where'd your ponytail go?" asked Megan sharply.

"I left it in the barber shop," Dad said with a chuckle.

"Can they put it back on?" asked Megan.

"No. I let them keep it."

"I want to give it to Natalie. She'd like it."

A muscle jumped in Dad's jaw as he looked helplessly at Mom. She shrugged, then ran to him and threw her arms around him.

"I think you look absolutely gorgeous!" Mom said.

He bent down and kissed her. "Thank you."

Just then Duke walked in and stopped short. He shot a startled look at Kathy. With a question in his eyes he motioned to Dad.

"It's Dad," Kathy said giggling.

"No!" Duke sprang forward. "Dad! You finally got your hair cut!"

Dad turned from Mom and playfully punched Duke in the arm. "Now we look alike."

Kathy looked at them standing side by side. Dad was taller and older, of course, but the two did look alike.

"So why'd you finally do it?" asked Duke as he

leaned back against the counter with his arms crossed over his chest.

"Let's all sit down and I'll tell you." Dad kissed Mom again, then sat on his chair at the table.

Kathy held her breath as the others sat down. She felt excitement and tension in the air. Just why had Dad made such a drastic change in his looks?

"Am I going to want to hear this, Tommy?" Mom asked.

"Yes, Grace."

Kathy let out her breath and leaned forward.

Dad looked around the table at each one. "I have been given the job as lead musician on the new Christian talk show on Channel 15."

"That's fantastic!" cried Mom while Kathy, Duke, and Megan cheered happily.

"You'll be on TV?" asked Kathy in awe.

"Wait'll I tell the guys," said Duke, grinning at Dad.

Dad looked very proud of himself. "They wanted my talent, but wanted to present a clean-cut, all-American look. I said I could part with the pony-tail and the ragged look. So I start tomorrow! The pay is great!" He named it off as he smiled at Mom.

Kathy gasped. Maybe now they could afford to hire a baby-sitter for Megan!

"So if you want to quit tutoring you can, Grace. We won't need that income," Dad said.

Kathy hadn't thought about Mom not wanting to tutor.

"What about your students?" asked Mom.

Dad flung his arms wide. "I am going to quit!"

Kathy blinked in surprise. She thought Dad loved teaching.

"Will you drop *all* your students?" asked Mom in surprise.

Dad shrugged. "I probably will keep Marcy and Linc. They're outstanding musicians and a pleasure to work with."

Kathy frowned as she realized both Mom and Dad would be gone almost every day. "Does that mean I have to watch Megan all the time?" she asked.

Dad shook his head. "No. But you'll still watch her on Tuesdays. After this week I'll be home every Monday and Wednesday. And I'll only have students on Monday."

"And I'll be home Thursdays and Fridays, the same as usual," said Mom.

"So, Kit Kat, it looks like you'll be baby-sitting only Tuesdays after this week," said Dad. "You will have her all day tomorrow though."

Kathy glanced at Duke, then at Dad. "Why can't Duke watch her tomorrow? Why can't we take turns after that?"

"No way!" said Duke with a firm shake of his head.

"Natalie will watch me," said Megan as she settled back in her chair and folded her arms. "She loves me."

Shame washed over Kathy. She took Megan's hand and smiled at her. "It's all right. I'll watch you, Megan."

4

Strange Happenings

Wednesday morning Kathy walked through the quiet house. Megan was outdoors in the sandbox, and everyone else was gone. Mom had said Billie McCrea, Chelsea's mom, was going to check on them off and on through the day. Billie and Mom had become best friends, much to Kathy's surprise. Mom had never had a best friend before. It was funny to think of two mothers sharing secrets and giggling together.

Kathy glanced out the window to check on Megan in the sandbox. The sandbox was empty! Megan was gone! "Not again!" Kathy cried as she dashed to the back door, through the garage, and out to the backyard. A warm wind brought the smell of a freshly baked pie from the house behind them.

"Megan!" shouted Kathy. "Where are you?"

"Right here," Megan called as she swung back and forth on her swing set.

Kathy sighed in relief.

Megan's ponytails flipped as she swung. She wore a pink sunsuit and white sandals. "Is it time to get Natalie yet?"

"Not yet. After your nap, remember?"

"Oh, yes. Now I remember."

"I'm going to water Mrs. Sobol's plants. Want to come with me?"

"Sure." Megan jumped off her swing and ran to Kathy. "I think that man already watered them."

"What man?" asked Kathy as they walked around to the side of the house and over into Mrs. Sobol's yard.

"The man who went in her house," said Megan.

Kathy knew Megan was making up another story. Mom said it was as natural for Megan to tell stories as it was for Dad to create music.

Kathy walked past the bench near the garage, past the flower bed, and to the side door. The key was hidden in the pot of a hanging plant. She reached up into the pot and felt around. She couldn't find the key. She brushed off her dirty fingers. "That's funny." She pulled a step-stool close, climbed on it, and peered into the pot. The key was gone. "She probably forgot to put it there when she left," muttered Kathy as she put the stool back in place. But it didn't matter. She knew a secret way to get in. Mrs. Sobol had showed her.

"That man took the key," said Megan as she followed Kathy to the front porch. It was a narrow porch with room only for a chair and a few plants.

Kathy carefully took the screen off the window in back of the chair, then pushed the window open. She moved the curtain and climbed in.

"I want to come too," Megan said, poking her head through the window.

Kathy helped her in, then closed the window. A hint of coffee hung in the air. "Stay with me, Megan. I don't want you accidentally breaking anything."

Kathy filled the watering can, then carefully watered the row of plants in the kitchen window. She turned, then frowned as she spotted a pile of mail on Mrs. Sobol's table. "That's funny," she muttered. Then she shrugged. Maybe it was yesterday's mail. She finished watering the flowers in the other rooms, put the can away in the pantry, then checked the mailbox at the front door. It was empty. Maybe the mailman hadn't come yet. She told Megan to wait on the porch, closed the door, making sure it was locked, then put the window screen back in place.

Later while Megan was taking her nap Kathy walked listlessly through their house. She wasn't allowed to watch daytime TV. The house seemed very quiet. Usually sounds of Dad's practice or his students' playing drifted through the whole house. Billie McCrea had called three times already to check on them, so Kathy knew she wouldn't call again. Later, after Megan woke up, Chelsea, Roxie, and Hannah were coming over so they could all go visit Betina again.

Kathy touched her *I'm A Best Friend* button. Her best friends were probably still working on a job. She'd had to call Roxie this morning to have someone else take over the job she was supposed to do. Roxie had said she wouldn't have any problem finding someone to do it.

Listlessly Kathy stopped at the window and looked out at Mrs. Sobol's house. A curtain fluttered at the living room window. Kathy froze. Chills ran up and down her back. Had she seen right? Had the curtain moved? Maybe it was just her imagination. She stood very still, barely breathing, and watched the window. The curtain didn't move. "It *was* my imagination!" Kathy said sharply to herself as she abruptly turned away.

Just then she heard a door close softly. Her heart skipped a beat. Was someone in their house? She remembered her special Scripture. "Fear, you don't belong to me!" she whispered. "God gave me power and love and a sound mind!"

With her head high she walked to the living room and called, "Mom?"

"It's me," said Duke.

Relieved that it wasn't some stranger, she stopped just inside the living room. "Why'd you use the front door?"

He shrugged. "It was closer."

"Oh."

"Where is everybody?"

"Megan's taking a nap. You know where Mom and Dad are. What's wrong with you, Duke?"

"I don't know." He rubbed his hands up and down his jeans. Sweat stood on his upper lip and across his forehead. "I guess I'm scared."

Kathy dropped to the edge of the couch. "Scared? Of what?"

"I thought I saw someone in Mrs. Sobol's house."

Kathy gasped. "Just now?"

"Yes." Duke sank down on Dad's favorite chair and gripped the arms of it. "I know I really didn't, but it sure seemed like it."

"I thought I saw the curtain in the living room move," whispered Kathy.

Duke blew out his breath. "Maybe we should check it out."

"Alone?"

Duke grinned. "We could take Megan."

Kathy giggled.

"Are we ready to go get Natalie?" asked Megan from the doorway. Her cheeks were flushed and her hair tangled. A sandal dangled from each hand.

"Will you stop talking about Natalie?" shouted Duke, jumping up. "You know she's not real!"

Megan's eyes filled with tears. She ran to Kathy and buried her face in Kathy's lap.

Kathy frowned at Duke.

"I'm sorry," he whispered as he sat back down. "Stop crying, Megan. I won't yell at you again."

Megan lifted her head and wiped away her tears. She crawled on the couch and dropped her sandals in Kathy's lap. "Natalie is my friend. So there."

Duke sank back with a groan.

Kathy buckled on Megan's sandals, then sent her to the bathroom. "When you get back, we'll go outdoors and wait for the girls."

"Where are you going?" asked Duke.

"To get Natalie," said Megan, holding her chin high as she walked away.

"To see Betina Quinn," Kathy corrected. "We told her we'd be back today."

"Could I go with you?"

"You? You never want to go anywhere with me."

Duke shrugged.

"Sure, you can go. But if Betina doesn't want you, you'll have to leave. She gets scared easily."

Duke rubbed his hand across his face. "It sure

did look like a man's face in Mrs. Sobol's window."

"Let's check it out before we leave," Kathy said, jumping up. "We don't have to be afraid."

A few minutes later Kathy rang Mrs. Sobol's back doorbell while Duke and Megan waited beside her. She listened for footsteps, but heard nothing. She pressed the doorbell again.

"Let's go inside," Duke said as he reached up to get the key from the pot.

"It's not there," said Kathy.

Duke lifted the key out. "It's right here."

Kathy gasped. "It wasn't there before."

"You probably just couldn't feel it."

"I even looked."

Duke pushed the key into the lock and turned it. "Shall we go in?"

"Hurry up!" Megan said. "I want to get Natalie."

Kathy watched Duke push the door open.

"Anybody here?" called Duke.

No one answered.

Kathy looked past Duke. She saw the table, but there wasn't anything on it. The pile of mail lay on the counter near the toaster. She shivered. "Megan, did you take Mrs. Sobol's mail off the table and put it on the counter when we were here a while ago?"

"Yes," Megan said. "She doesn't want stuff on her table. She always tells me that."

Kathy laughed in relief. She was making a mystery out of nothing. "Lock up and put the key back, Duke. I think we both imagined things."

"I guess so." Duke locked the door and put the key back in the hanging pot.

They walked back to their yard and sat in the grass in the shade of a tall maple to wait for the girls.

"Are you sure you want to go with us, Duke?" asked Kathy. She couldn't imagine him doing that.

"Don't you want me to go?" he asked gruffly.

"Sure, you can go. I'm just surprised you want to."

"You can't yell at Natalie," said Megan, shaking her finger at Duke.

"I won't," he said, rolling his eyes.

Kathy studied Duke thoughtfully. Finally she said, "Did Dad tell you to go with us?"

Duke flushed and nodded.

"I should've known," Kathy said impatiently.

"But I do want to go . . . Really . . . I want to see Betina Quinn and her estate."

"And Natalie," said Megan.

Duke grabbed Megan and tickled her until she giggled hard.

Kathy laughed as she watched them. Maybe it would be fun to have Duke along.

5

The Visit

At Betina Quinn's estate Kathy stood back with her friends and Duke while Megan ran to the French doors and peered inside.

"She might not let us stay today," whispered Roxie.

"I hope she doesn't," said Duke.

Kathy frowned at him, and he frowned right back at her.

"My mom says she used to go to church all the time before her husband and little girl were killed," Hannah said.

"I feel sorry for her," Chelsea said softly.

"Here she comes!" cried Megan, laughing as she bounced up and down.

Kathy locked her fingers together and waited. Birds sang in the trees. An airplane flew high across the bright blue sky.

Betina opened the door and stepped out. She

wore the same baggy gray T-shirt and faded jeans, but her hair was brushed back and held in a ponytail with a wide yellow band. She bent down and hugged Megan. "Hi," she said softly.

"My dad got his ponytail cut off," Megan announced as she caught Betina's hand with both of hers. "I wanted him to give it to Natalie, but he said the barber kept it."

Kathy laughed under her breath. She'd told her friends about Dad's new look and new job. They were happy about both.

Finally Betina turned to face the others. She gasped, and the color drained from her face when she saw Duke. "Who . . . who is that?" she whispered.

"Oh, that's just Duke," said Megan.

"He's our brother," Kathy said. "Duke, this is Betina Quinn."

"I'm happy to meet you," Duke said with a shaky smile.

Betina nodded briefly, then turned back to Megan.

"We want to see all your beds," Megan said.

"Megan!" said Kathy with a warning frown.

Megan ignored Kathy and asked Betina, "Where did Natalie sleep last night?"

Duke groaned.

"In the room across from mine," Betina said.

Kathy stepped forward to stop the talk about

Natalie. "Your house is big and beautiful. Would you show it to us, please?"

Betina hesitated, then nodded.

"Thank you!" the girls all cried at once. Duke looked bored.

Kathy's heart fluttered as they followed Betina through the French doors into a huge room with comfortable chairs, couches, a fireplace, a big-screen TV, and plants everywhere. The plants badly needed water. Dust covered the plants and the furniture. Kathy glanced at Chelsea and knew she was trying to find a way to talk to Betina about the *King's Kids* working for her.

Betina led the way through the house, opening doors so the others could look inside. Every room was full of beautiful furniture covered with a thick layer of dust. The kitchen was clean in a spot where Betina fixed her meals, but the rest was dusty. Her bedroom was somewhat clean, but the other eight bedrooms were so dusty Kathy sneezed over and over. Betina opened the bedroom door across from hers, then leaned against the wall without glancing inside.

Megan ran into the room, and the others followed. It was a little girl's room with stuffed animals and a white canopy bed.

Kathy glanced around the room. Tears stung the backs of her eyes as she thought of Betina's little girl. Kathy caught Megan's arm. "Don't touch anything," Kathy whispered. "It might make Betina feel bad."

"It's so sad," whispered Hannah, and the others agreed. For once Megan was silent.

A few minutes later as they walked down the wide stairs Megan said, "Betina, your house sure is dirty."

Kathy flushed with embarrassment. She saw Duke's face turn red and knew he wanted to snap at Megan, but he didn't.

"It is?" Betina looked around with a slight frown. "I never noticed." At the bottom of the steps she ran a finger over a small table with a tall vase on it. Dust coated her finger, and she stared at it as if she'd never seen dust before. "You're right, Megan."

Smiling, Chelsea stepped forward. "We would be glad to clean for you." She held out the ad for *King's Kids*.

Betina scanned the ad. "I don't know," she said vaguely.

"We won't do anything you don't want us to do," Kathy told her.

"Would Megan come with you?" asked Betina.

"Sure," said Megan, grinning.

"We'd have to ask our parents," Duke added.

"You can't come if she doesn't come," snapped Betina.

"I'll come," said Megan, tapping her thin chest with her fingertips.

Kathy laughed with the others. Duke frowned.

"Dad'll let me," Megan said.

Betina stroked Megan's hair.

"I'll mow the lawn," Duke offered.

Kathy stared at him in surprise. He'd signed up with the *King's Kids*, but so far he hadn't accepted a single job. Was he doing it now because Dad had said to keep an eye on them while they were with Betina Quinn? Kathy studied Duke thoughtfully. Was there danger that she wasn't aware of?

Betina crossed her arms and rubbed her hands up and down her thin arms. "I don't want people around."

"It'll just be us," Hannah said gently.

Kathy thought of the huge house and wondered if they could even do the job. She watched Betina try to make up her mind. Without warning Kathy sneezed, then sneezed again. "Sorry," she muttered.

"It's the dust," Betina said sharply. She lifted her chin and looked very determined. "Yes! Yes, you can clean for me." She pointed at Duke. "And you can mow the lawn."

"I'll work on your flower beds," Chelsea said. "I'm good with flowers."

"She worked on my mom's flowers when they looked terrible," said Roxie. "Now they're beautiful, and she just might win the Prettiest Flowers Contest."

Betina nodded at Chelsea. "You can take care of the flowers."

"And what can I do?" asked Megan eagerly.

Betina stroked Megan's cheek. "You can sit on the swing with me and talk to me."

"No, I mean real work. I saw all those toys in your little girl's room. I could clean them."

Betina sagged against the newel post. "I don't have a little girl," she whispered raggedly.

Kathy bit her lip. She wanted to grab Megan and make her close her mouth.

"Your little girl went to be with Jesus . . . my dad told me," Megan said. "But she didn't take her toys. You can't take toys and things to Heaven with you 'cause you don't need 'em there. Jesus already has all the stuff for you you'll want."

Tears filled Betina's eyes. "Go away!" she snapped. "I don't want you here!"

Megan jumped back in surprise.

Kathy slipped her arm around Megan. "Let's go."

"We'll be back tomorrow to work," Chelsea said.

Betina shook her head hard. Her ponytail whipped across her thin back. "No! Don't ever *ever* come back!"

"Let's go, girls," Duke said, heading for the door.

Megan pulled away from Kathy and stepped right up to Betina. "Why are you mad at us?"

Betina's chin quivered. "Please go," she whispered hoarsely.

"Did you think we were going to hurt you?" asked Megan.

"Shhh, Megan," Kathy said, reaching for her little sister. "Let's go."

Megan pushed Kathy's hand down and moved another step closer to Betina. "Want me to leave Natalie another night with you?"

"Megan!" snapped Duke. "Come on!"

Betina turned on Duke, her eyes flashing. "Don't you say one harsh word to that child!"

Duke's face and neck turned scarlet. He looked helplessly at Kathy, then down at the floor.

"He doesn't like Natalie," whispered Megan to Betina. "He's just mad because I talked about her."

Betina touched Megan's cheek with the tips of her fingers. "I'm sorry I got upset. Come back tomorrow." She looked at the others. "You all come back tomorrow."

"We will," Kathy said.

"Even you," Betina said, looking right at Duke.

He barely nodded.

Betina kissed Megan's cheek. "Run along now."

Megan hugged Betina, then skipped across the room with the others following her.

Kathy hesitated, then hurried after them, her heart hammering against her rib cage. Her nose itched, and she rubbed it. No one spoke until they were on the sidewalk outside the brick wall that ran along the front of the estate.

"I don't want to go back there ever again," Duke said gruffly.

"I'm going back," the girls all said together. Then they giggled because they'd said the same thing at the time time.

Suddenly Megan stopped. "I forgot Natalie!"

"Leave her there," snapped Duke, then flushed. "You can't forget something that isn't real."

Kathy caught Megan's hand and held on tight as she tried to pull free. "Betina doesn't want us to go back right now. She's feeling sad about her little girl."

Megan stopped tugging and nodded. "And Natalie will be her friend again tonight."

Duke groaned.

"But I don't want her to keep Natalie forever." Megan's eyes filled with tears. "I need a best friend, you know."

"I know." Kathy kissed Megan's cheek. "Let's get home and help Mom make dinner."

6

The New Job

Kathy wheeled her bike up to the Crandalls' three-car garage and jumped off. Today they were to start their new job. She'd agreed to meet the girls there at 10, but she was late because she'd overslept. Last night Megan had crawled into bed with her because she didn't have Natalie to keep her company. Kathy hadn't slept well at all.

Kathy ran to the side door and rang the bell. She tucked her pink shirt into her pink shorts and tightened the pink leather belt. Gracie, the little dog that belonged to Ezra Menski, barked and ran back to her own yard next door.

Hannah answered the door with a glad smile. Somewhere in the house two dogs barked. "You're just in time," Hannah said. "Chelsea's assigning jobs."

Stifling a yawn, Kathy followed Hannah through the hall to the kitchen. It was a small room flooded with sunshine. Everything looked clean and tidy. It would be easy to keep it that way. "Sorry I'm late," she said, smiling at Chelsea and Roxie.

"No big deal," said Chelsea with a slight frown.

"What's wrong?" asked Roxie.

"I just realized that I didn't see *both* cats this morning." Chelsea brushed back her red hair. "Did you girls notice?"

"I saw the black one," Roxie said.

"So did I," Hannah added.

"But not the white one." Chelsea cupped her hands around her mouth and called, "Here, kitty. Kitty, kitty. Here, kitty."

The black cat streaked across the tiled floor and meowed up at Chelsea.

"Where's the white cat?" asked Chelsea with a worried frown. "We'd better look through the house just in case she's shut in a room and can't get out." Chelsea assigned different parts of the house to each girl.

Kathy hurried upstairs. The five bedrooms were her assigned rooms. Voices floated up behind her. She opened the first closet in the hallway. It smelled like cedar. A fur coat hung inside, along with two wool coats. The cat wasn't there. She checked the bedrooms carefully, looking under the beds and inside the closets. In the last bedroom she heard a slight noise from inside the closet. The closet door was open, so Kathy cautiously peered inside. On a folded quilt on the floor she saw the white cat nursing five tiny newborn kittens.

With a low laugh Kathy crouched down and carefully put her hand out to the white cat. The cat looked at Kathy, but didn't move. She rubbed the cat's head, then gently stroked the white kittens one at a time. "You're so cute and soft," she whispered. Finally she ran downstairs, calling to the girls as she ran.

"I found her!" Kathy shouted again when no one came. "Chelsea! Roxie! Hannah! I found the cat!"

"Kathy found the cat!" Chelsea shouted from somewhere in the house.

Kathy waited impatiently at the bottom of the stairs until the girls ran to her. "You'll love it!" she cried. "Follow me." She led the way to the bedroom. She opened the closet door wider. "Look!"

"Ohhh!" Chelsea dropped to her knees.

Roxie and Hannah pushed in to get a better look at the kittens. "They're so cute!" whispered Hannah.

"I want one," said Roxie, gently touching a kitten. "I wonder if they'll give them away."

Chelsea stroked the white cat. "Mrs. Crandall didn't tell me you were expecting kittens." She glanced back at Kathy. "Let's find a basket and take them to the laundry room."

Kathy found a wicker laundry basket in a corner of the bedroom. She lined it with light blue towels and set it near the closet. She watched as Chelsea carefully moved the kittens to their new home. They looked even smaller in the basket. The white cat walked back and forth as if she was worried, then jumped in the basket and settled down with her kittens. She licked each one as if she was making sure they were safe.

"Yuk! Look at the quilt," said Roxie, wrinkling her nose. The quilt had a few strange-looking and strange-smelling spots on it. "We'll have to wash it." She gingerly picked it up, actually touching the quilt as little as possible. "I wonder if it's safe to wash this."

"I think so," Hannah said as she looked it over. "We'll wash it in cold water."

Kathy held one handle of the basket and Chelsea the other. Walking slowly and carefully, as though they were carrying a hundred eggs, they carried it downstairs to the laundry room. They set it in the opposite corner from the litter box.

Roxie filled the washing machine with cold water, added detergent, then carefully put the quilt in.

As the washer sloshed the quilt, the girls knelt around the basket and watched the newborns. The cute kittens made tiny mewing sounds that the girls found most entertaining.

"I never saw a kitten being born," Kathy said softly. "Have you?"

They all shook their heads.

"I saw a baby born on TV once," Roxie said. "It's funny to think of a baby growing inside his mother, isn't it?"

Hannah said, "When I look at baby Burke I can't believe he has toenails and fingernails and everything! He's a whole complete human being, just tiny."

"I remember when Megan was born," Kathy said just above a whisper. "She was so small! I was jealous of her for a long time." Kathy flushed. "I never told anybody that before!"

Chelsea sighed heavily. "I was mad when Mike was born. I wanted a sister, not another brother! Sometimes I'm still mad."

Hannah bit her lip. "Sometimes I'm mad because I'm not white like you girls. I know I'm supposed to be proud of who I am, but I'm not always. Sometimes I'm mad about being Native American."

"I never thought of you as being different," said Kathy.

"I did," Roxie said. "But it doesn't matter now that we're friends."

Hannah pulled a paper from the pocket of her blue shorts. "Mom gave me a Scripture she said was special for me. I think you girls would like it too." She smoothed out the paper. "Psalm 139:4. 'I will praise God; for I am fearfully and wonderfully made.'"

Kathy touched her tight blonde curls. "I should be happy about my hair then, shouldn't I?"

"And I should be glad I have freckles," Chelsea said, wrinkling her nose.

"And I shouldn't be mad because I have a talent to carve," Roxie commented seriously. "Ever since Grandma gave me Grandpa's wood carving tools I've felt bad about not using them. I hate having a special talent! I don't want to carve!"

"I'd like to have a special talent," Kathy said. All her life she'd been around special talent—Dad's music . . . and Megan's imagination and storytelling ever since she'd been old enough to talk.

Hannah smoothed the paper again and sighed heavily. "And none of us should be mad because of our brothers and sisters. They are fearfully and wonderfully made too."

Kathy thought about Megan, then Duke. Could she praise God for them? Oh, it would be so hard!

The girls were quiet for a long time. Finally Chelsea said, "I guess we'd better get to work. We all have jobs later today."

"I heard more about Betina Quinn," Hannah said before they could move.

A chill ran down Kathy's spine. "What?"

"My dad said that before the accident Betina's

husband, Jason, called him and wanted to talk. Mr. Quinn said he and Betina had just had a major fight."

"What about?" asked Roxie.

Hannah absently scratched the white cat's neck. "Jason Quinn wanted them to adopt a boy and a girl who needed a home. Betina didn't want their little girl to have to share their love with adopted children, so she said no. They were still fighting about it when Jason and their daughter Carlene were killed."

"That's so sad," Kathy said with tears in her eyes.

"Betina probably can't forgive her husband or herself," Chelsea stated. "I know how hard forgiving others can be."

Kathy dashed her tears away and slowly stood. "We can tell Betina Jesus will help her forgive Jason and forgive herself."

"Then she can be happy again," Hannah said.

The girls slowly walked back to the kitchen. Kathy looked out the window as she silently prayed for Betina. Just then the phone rang, and Kathy almost jumped out of her skin.

Chelsea answered the phone, listened a minute, then held the phone out to Kathy. "It's your mom."

Kathy's heart sank as she reached for the phone. It could mean only one thing: Mom needed her to baby-sit Megan again. "Hi, Mom."

"Kathy, I just received a call from one of my students. He can't meet at our regular time and asked if I could come now. I need you to come watch Megan."

Kathy's temper flared. "I'm working, Mom. Why can't Duke do it?"

"He's not here, and I don't know how to reach him. I'm sorry, Kath. Please hurry, would you?"

A muscle jumped in Kathy's jaw. She kept her voice even as she said, "Sure, Mom." She hung up, then stamped her foot hard. "I have to baby-sit! Again! It's just not fair! How I wish Megan had never been born! I wish she was dead just like Betina's little girl!" Kathy clamped her hand over her mouth and stared at the others with wide eyes.

With a whimper she ran from the house, grabbed her bike, and pedaled away as fast as she could go. Her terrible words rang over and over in her ears and sounded worse each time she heard them.

7

Duke

Kathy took a deep breath, let it out in one rush, then walked into her house. The smell of disinfectant turned her stomach. "I'm home, Mom!"

"Oh, good. I'm very sorry I had to do this." Mom hurried past, her purse in one hand, her keys and briefcase in the other. "I'll be back as soon as I can. Megan's watching *Cinderella* again."

Kathy slowly walked to the living room. She couldn't look at Megan. How could she be so awful as to actually wish Megan was dead? She was the worst person in the whole world! And now her best friends knew it! They'd never want to see her or talk to her again now that they knew what she was really like. She moaned and tried hard to blink away her tears but couldn't.

"Did you get hurt, Kathy?" asked Megan, looking over her shoulder at Kathy.

"No," she whispered. She'd have to be extra-nice to Megan to hide how she really felt. "Want to go to the park and finish watching *Cinderella* later?"

"Yes! Yes, Kathy!" Megan jumped up and clicked off the VCR and TV. "You're the best sister in the whole world!"

Kathy's heart froze. "Run to the bathroom, then we'll go."

Megan ran to the bathroom just as Duke walked in.

"Where's Mom?"

Kathy told him. "Now that you're home, you can watch Megan so I can go back to work."

Duke shook his head. "No way! Mom told you to."

Kathy doubled her fists in anger toward Duke. "You always get out of it! Just where do you go when you leave and nobody can find you?"

Duke flushed hotly. "None of your business, Kathy Aber!"

"Are you two fighting again?" asked Megan from the doorway. She looked ready to cry.

"She started it," Duke said, jabbing his finger at Kathy.

She forced her temper down. "I'm not fighting now. We're going to the park."

"The park?" asked Duke in a strangled voice as the color drained from his face.

Kathy frowned impatiently. "What's wrong with that? We always go to the park."

"Let's go," said Megan, tugging Kathy's hand. "Want to come, Duke?"

"Sure," he said gruffly.

"You can swing me," Megan said, skipping toward the door.

Kathy shot Duke a shocked look. Why was he afraid to go to the park, and why was he going with them even though he was afraid?

Duke ducked out the door before Kathy could say anything. She didn't want to argue with him in front of Megan anyway. It always upset Megan when they fought.

At the park Megan sat on the swing, and Duke pushed her. Kathy stood to one side and watched Duke through her long lashes. He kept looking around as if he was looking for someone. Was this a mystery? If so, Hannah would be able to solve it. Kathy's heart sank. She couldn't call Hannah after her own terrible outburst a while ago.

Just then Duke's face turned as white as the clouds in the sky.

Kathy shot a look around to see what or who had frightened Duke. She saw two boys Duke's age near the pond and several kids playing ball. A few adults sat on benches watching small children in the sandbox.

"Push me, Duke," said Megan impatiently as she kicked her feet up and down.

Duke pushed Megan again, but he wasn't paying attention to how high.

Kathy tried to imagine what was wrong with Duke, but she couldn't figure it out. He'd quit telling her things about himself when he was in first grade and she was in kindergarten. For a long time that hurt her feelings, and then she stopped caring.

"Duke!" cried Megan. She squealed with fear. "Stop me! I'm going too high!"

Duke caught her and eased her to a stop. "Go play in the sandbox for a while."

Megan ran off without a backward glance. She settled in the sandbox and immediately started talking to the other kids there.

Duke pushed his hands into the pockets of his jeans and hunched his thin shoulders. A gust of wind ruffled his blond hair.

"What's wrong?" asked Kathy sharply.

Duke turned to her in surprise. "Oh . . . I forgot you were here."

She stepped closer to him. "Who are you afraid of?"

"Me? What makes you think that?"

"I was watching you."

His face darkened. "Leave me alone, Kathy."

"I was only asking," she said stiffly.

"Mind your own business!"

She doubled her fists and stepped even closer. "Just what are you hiding?"

He flushed to the roots of his hair. "Nothing!"

"I know better." Kathy narrowed her eyes. "I'm going to tell Dad something's wrong with you. He'll figure it out."

Duke gripped Kathy's arm. "Don't you dare say a single word to Dad!"

She jerked free and tried to rub away the pain. "What's wrong with you, Duke?"

"Nothing, I told you!"

"You're scaring me." She lowered her voice. "Are you in some kind of trouble?"

"What d' you mean?"

"Trouble like . . . I don't know!" She spread her hands wide. "You're a nice guy. What kind of trouble do nice guys get into?"

He glanced around, then cried out, "Where's Megan?"

Kathy's heart zoomed to her feet. She looked around, then finally saw her near the wishing well. "She's over there."

Duke ran toward Megan, calling frantically to her.

Kathy frowned. "What's wrong with him?" she muttered to herself. She watched him grab Megan's hand and walk her to the short slide. Slowly Kathy walked toward them. She watched Megan climb up the slide and swish down. Her laughter floated over to Kathy.

How could she ever wish her sweet little sister was dead?

Kathy forced back the horrible thought. She perched on the edge of a green bench near the slide and watched Duke and Megan play. A pigeon landed on the ground nearby, pecked a while, then flew away. Kathy couldn't remember Duke ever playing in the park with Megan unless the whole family was there together for a picnic or a walk. What was going on with him?

Just then a boy with long dark hair walked up to Duke. Kathy couldn't hear what they were saying, but she knew Duke was upset. Kathy slowly walked toward them. Maybe she could get close enough to hear them before Duke noticed her. Megan looked up and saw her, but Kathy put her finger to her lips to silence her. Her little sister covered her mouth with her hand to hide a giggle. Kathy knew Megan thought they were playing a game.

Kathy crept closer. She heard Duke call the boy Brody. She frowned thoughtfully. She'd heard the name before, but she couldn't remember what Duke had said about him.

"Cole said you better keep quiet," Brody said gruffly.

"I said I would," Duke snapped. "Now leave me alone."

"Cole knows what your sisters look like and where they live, you know," Brody said.

Kathy trembled. Brody was threatening Duke—and her and Megan! But why? Who was Cole?

Just then Duke glanced around and saw Kathy. His eyes widened in fear. He turned back, gripped Brody's arm, and pulled him away from the slide.

Kathy leaned weakly against the slide. Just what kind of trouble was Duke in? She'd have to tell Dad and let him take care of Duke before he got hurt. But what if her imagination was running wild? She had to call the Best Friends and talk it over with them. They'd tell her what to do.

Tears burned her eyes. She couldn't call them. Not now; maybe not ever.

Megan ran to Kathy and slipped her hand in hers. "Why are you sad?"

Kathy swallowed the lump in her throat.

"Don't be sad. I'm here." Megan patted Kathy's arm. "I'll make you feel better."

Kathy bent down and hugged Megan. Oh, how could she love Megan one minute and wish her dead the next? "Let's get Duke and go home," Kathy said, brushing away her tears.

"Race ya," called Megan, running toward Duke.

Laughing, Kathy ran after Megan.

"Duke!" called Megan. "We're going home."

Brody ran across the park, leaving Duke standing alone. Kathy watched Brody stop beside a man. They both looked back at Duke, then at her. She shivered. What was going on?

At home Kathy sent Megan to the backyard to play while she followed Duke to the kitchen, where he sat down at the table to eat a bowl of cornflakes. She sat down and leaned toward him. "I want to know what you're afraid of, Duke. I mean it! Why did Brody threaten you?" She sounded like a TV show!

Duke dropped his spoon with a clatter. "Mind your own business!"

"You *are* my business! You're my brother."

"What can you do? You're only a kid."

"Then tell Dad!"

Duke shook his head and groaned. "I don't dare."

Kathy jumped up and looked out the window to make sure Megan was there. She was playing in the sandbox. Relieved, Kathy sat down again. "Why are you scared? Tell me!"

Duke shivered. "I don't know how it happened, Kathy. Honest."

"Tell me!" Butterflies fluttered in her stomach.

"I've been . . . practicing guitar at . . . Brody's house."

Kathy frowned. "You told Dad you hate guitar."

"Well, I don't! I just don't want him to hear me play until I'm good." Duke pushed his bowl aside. "Dad is so good at everything, and I'm not."

"But Dad wasn't good when he first started learning to play."

"He couldn't have been as bad as me."

"What about Brody?" Kathy asked to get Duke back on the subject.

"I practice at his house. We play together, and I'm learning fast." Duke took a deep breath. "Last week Brody's brother Cole came in and listened to us. He joked around with us for a while. He gave Brody some drugs, then offered me some."

Kathy gasped. She'd never been around anyone who'd done that.

"I didn't take them, of course. I said I'd never do drugs. Brody laughed at me. I decided I'd never go back to his house again. Then he saw me in the park. I saw Cole dealing drugs there, and Brody knew I saw him. They said if I tell they'll hurt you and Megan."

Kathy fell back against her chair with a gasp. Would they really attack Duke or her or Megan? "You have to tell Dad! You have to, Duke!"

"I can't! He'll think I'm terrible for getting into so much trouble."

"He loves you, Duke!"

"Not like he loves you and Megan."

Kathy stared in shock at Duke. "How can you say that? You're his only son!"

"But you and Megan are his little girls."

Kathy helplessly shook her head. She'd never in all her life thought Duke would feel this way. Just then she thought about Megan, and she ran to peer out the window again. Megan was still in the sandbox. Kathy turned back to Duke. "Are you afraid Cole will come here and hurt me and Megan?"

"He might," whispered Duke.

Kathy ran to the door. "Then I'm staying right with Megan! Come on!"

Duke followed Kathy out, and they sat on the picnic table with their feet on the bench and watched Megan play in the sandbox.

"I better tell you the rest," Duke said hoarsely.

Kathy shivered. "The rest?"

"I think Cole has been in Mrs. Sobol's house."

"No!"

"I'm not positive, but I know I saw someone in there."

"I'm telling Dad the minute he gets home," said Kathy sharply. "I mean it."

Duke sighed heavily. "You're right, I guess. I sure can't handle it alone." He smiled slightly. "Thanks, Kath."

"You're welcome."

"I guess you're not so bad after all."

Kathy jabbed him in the ribs with her elbow. "Thanks a lot!"

Duke grinned. "I hate not having a brother, but I'm glad you're my sister."

Kathy stared at Duke in surprise. She'd never thought about him wanting a brother.

"Sometimes I even wish I was a girl so I'd fit in the family better," Duke said, flushing.

"You're kidding! Mom and Dad love you most because you're the only boy!"

Duke shook his head. "I don't believe that. I'm nothing! I don't have special talent like Dad. I'm not as smart as you. And I'm not the youngest or the cutest like Megan."

"Hannah read a Scripture to us today that you need to hear. I know it's in Psalms, but I can't remember where. But it says, 'I will praise God; for I am fearfully and wonderfully made.' Isn't that awesome?"

Duke thought about it a while and finally shrugged. "I guess I don't feel fearfully and wonderfully made though."

"It doesn't matter if you feel like it or not. You are anyway." Kathy laughed. She realized she liked talking with Duke. But it felt strange.

Megan ran to them and climbed up on the table. "What are we talking about?" she asked.

"*We* aren't talking about anything," said Kathy with a laugh. "Duke and I are."

Megan crawled in between Kathy and Duke. "Now we can talk."

"What about?" asked Duke.

"The man I saw at Mrs. Sobol's house," Megan said giggling.

Kathy froze as she stared in horror at Duke. Was Cole at Mrs. Sobol's house this very minute? Was he waiting to harm them?

8

Help

Kathy crept around to the front of their house with Duke and Megan behind her. They had to see if there was a man in Mrs. Sobol's house. Maybe it was only another one of Megan's stories . . . Or maybe it was Cole. They had to know.

"Be careful," Duke whispered.

"I am."

"Me too," said Megan in a loud whisper.

Kathy dashed across Mrs. Sobol's yard and up to her side door. Her heart thudded as she waited for Duke and Megan. Kathy's mouth felt bone-dry. She reached up into the hanging pot for the key. She felt dirt and a dried leaf, then finally the key. She trembled so much she almost dropped it.

Duke took the key and unlocked the door. He shivered. "I don't know if we should go in," he whispered.

"We have to see if anyone's in there." Kathy stepped closer to Duke. She smelled his sweat.

Megan reached out and pushed the door. The hinges creaked as it opened.

Kathy tensed, ready to grab Megan and run. The house felt empty. She followed Duke inside, and they stood in the kitchen and listened. She heard the hum of the refrigerator but nothing more.

"Anybody here?" shouted Megan.

Duke grabbed her and shushed her. She scowled at him, but kept quiet.

Kathy's legs shook as they walked through the house. It was indeed empty. She even looked in the attic where Mrs. Sobol had accidentally locked Chelsea in. It was hot and smelled closed in. No one was hiding in it. She locked it again, and they walked back downstairs, checked the garage and basement, then left.

In the yard Kathy took a deep breath. "We were scared for no reason."

Duke looked at the key in his hand. "Does this key look different to you?" he asked in a tense voice.

Frowning, Kathy studied it. "Different how?"

"The color."

"It's silver," said Kathy. She gasped, and her heart almost jumped through her T-shirt. "It was brass colored before."

"It's a copy," Duke whispered in a strangled voice. "Someone exchanged keys!"

Kathy darted a look around, fearful someone was waiting and watching and ready to pounce on them. "Let's get home quick!" She grabbed Megan's hand and ran for their own house.

Duke closed and locked their front door. Sweat stood out on his face.

Megan looked from Duke to Kathy and back again. "We don't have to be afraid. We got angels watching over us."

"You're right!" Kathy turned to Duke. "She's right."

Duke nodded, but he didn't unlock their door.

The phone rang, shattering the silence. Kathy shrieked and jumped, then ran to answer it. It was Hannah. Kathy quickly dropped the receiver in place with a clatter. She turned away from the phone, her face white.

"What?" Duke asked in alarm.

"It was Hannah," whispered Kathy.

Duke frowned. "Your friend?"

Kathy nodded while she struggled to hold back tears.

"But why wouldn't you talk with her? That's not like you at all, Kathy."

Kathy doubled her fists at her sides and spat, "How do you know, Duke Aber? You don't even know me!"

"Don't fight again," said Megan, clutching at one, then the other.

Kathy struggled with her anger and finally got it under control. "Sorry," she whispered.

Duke raked his fingers through his short blond hair. "I told you my problem—now you tell me yours."

Kathy glanced at Megan and quickly away. "I can't."

Pain crossed Duke's face, but he quickly hid it. "So keep your secrets. See if I care!"

Kathy had seen Duke's pain. He really was interested in her story! Maybe she should tell him. She bent down to Megan. "You can watch the rest of *Cinderella* if you want."

Megan clung to Kathy's hand and looked up at her with wide brown eyes that were suddenly filling with tears. "Don't fight with Duke. If you're nice to him, I'll go watch *Cinderella*."

Kathy's heart turned over. "I'll be nice to him," she whispered around the lump in her throat.

Megan hugged Kathy, then Duke. She laughed happily and ran to the living room, her long pony-tails dancing across her shoulders.

Kathy walked slowly to the kitchen table and sat down. She rubbed her hand over her curls. They flattened, then sprang back up. "I'll tell you," she whispered.

Duke sat on the edge of a chair across the table

from Kathy. "I promise not to tell if you don't want me to."

She turned the lazy susan around and around. Finally she looked up. "You'll hate me when you hear."

Duke scowled. "I will not!"

Kathy took a deep breath and told him in a low tight voice how she felt about taking care of Megan and what she'd said right out loud for her friends to hear. "And now I can't ever see them again. They must hate me for sure."

"I can't believe that. They're your best friends." Duke locked his fingers together. "Best friends! I don't have a best friend. Do you know that?"

"I guess I never thought about it."

"Rob McCrea is nice, but he doesn't have time for me since I don't know about computers. And Brody . . . Brody does drugs. I won't ever go to his house again. Not even to practice guitar with him."

"I wouldn't either." Kathy shuddered.

Duke sighed heavily. Finally he said, "So what'll you tell your friends when it's time to go to Betina Quinn's?"

Kathy slapped her forehead. "I'd forgotten we're going back this afternoon. Maybe Hannah was calling to make some excuse for not going with me."

The door opened, and Mom walked in with Dad right behind her.

"Sorry to be so long," Mom said. She stopped in the middle of the room and studied Duke and Kathy. "What's wrong? Where's Megan?"

"Watching *Cinderella*," said Kathy.

Mom rushed to the living room, and Dad pulled out a chair and sat down. It was hard to get used to his short hair and dress clothes.

"Out with it, you two," Dad said firmly but kindly. "It looks like whatever it is, it's more than two kids can handle."

Kathy and Duke looked at each other. "You first, Duke," Kathy whispered.

Duke blanched. "I didn't mean for it to happen, Dad."

"Just tell me, son. I'm here to help." Dad squeezed Duke's arm and smiled.

Duke took a deep breath, let it out, and started his story. He ended by telling about the silver key they'd found in Mrs. Sobol's plant. "I'm not sure Cole's been in there, but he might have."

Dad tugged at the collar of his white shirt. "I guess the first step is to call Pedro Rodriguez at the police station. He's been working on a drug case, so he might already know about Cole." Dad stabbed his fingers through his hair. "As for Mrs. Sobol's house, I guess we'll have to keep a closer eye on it. I don't want you kids to go there alone again, not even to water her plants."

Kathy nodded thankfully.

Dad strode to the kitchen phone and called Pedro Rodriguez. As quickly as he could, he told the police officer all that Duke had told him.

Kathy watched Dad's face as he listened to Pedro's response. A shiver ran down her spine.

Finally Dad hung up and turned with a wide smile. "Thanks to you, Duke, Pedro will watch Cole more closely. He's suspected Cole was dealing drugs. After he's arrested I'm going to have a talk with Brody. I don't want him following in his brother's footsteps."

"He might listen to you," Duke said. "You're almost his idol because of how you play guitar."

"I'm glad he recognizes talent when he sees it," Dad said with a chuckle.

Kathy giggled.

Dad sat at the table again and turned to Kathy. "It's your turn."

Kathy sagged low in her seat. How could she tell Dad how really bad she was?

Mom walked in with Megan. Mom said cheerfully, "Who's ready for lunch? We're hungry, and we thought you might be too."

Kathy sighed in relief.

"We'll talk later," Dad said for her ears alone.

Her heart sank.

After a lunch of grilled cheese sandwiches, sliced peaches, and a glass of milk, Kathy walked listlessly across the backyard. Shade from the large trees protected her from the hot sun. Birds sang in the trees. In the distance a car honked. Kathy sank to the picnic bench and sighed with boredom. Duke was in his room, and Mom and Megan were both taking naps.

"We came to talk to you, Kathy."

She leaped up, and her heart zoomed to her feet as Chelsea, Hannah, and Roxie walked toward her. She wanted to run inside and lock the door behind her.

"Please don't run," Hannah said softly.

"We want to talk," Chelsea urged gently.

Roxie took a step forward. "We know you didn't mean what you said."

Kathy sighed and sank back on the bench. Giant tears filled her eyes. "But I did mean it," she whispered. "I'm rotten! I'm really really bad!"

The girls swarmed around her, all talking at once. Finally Chelsea called for order.

"We'll talk one at a time," she said. "I'll start since I've felt the same way about my little brother Mike."

Kathy gasped and wiped at her eyes. "You did?"

"I never admitted it to anyone because it was so terrible." Chelsea smiled weakly. "I guess if you're rotten, then so am I."

"Me too," said Hannah, hanging her head.

"I guess I really don't hate Megan," Kathy said

as she absently picked at her thumbnail. "She says and does so many cute things. It's just that I get so tired of watching her!"

"Why don't you talk to your parents about it?" asked Roxie.

"I tried," Kathy said. "But I couldn't say what I really felt."

"Try again," Chelsea said.

Kathy thought about it for a long time and finally nodded. "I will." Dad planned to have a serious talk with her that night. She'd tell him then.

The back door slammed, and Duke walked out. He stopped in surprise when he saw the girls.

"Come join us, Duke," Kathy called, surprising herself more than anyone. She realized she really did want him to join them, and that surprised her even more.

Slowly Duke walked over to them. "What's up?" he asked hesitantly.

"We were just talking," Chelsea told him with a shrug.

"They don't hate me," Kathy said, smiling at Duke.

He smiled back. "I told you." He turned to Roxie. "I read about the Art Fair at the park in September. Are you going to take your carvings and sell them?"

Roxie flushed and shook her head.

"Why not?" asked Hannah. "You're good!"

"I only have the mouse carved," Roxie said weakly.

Kathy squeezed Roxie's hand. "You have time to do more."

"I wish I had your talent," Chelsea said, sighing. "I'd carve things to sell and get out of debt quicker."

"Everybody will compare me with Mom and Grandpa," Roxie whispered. "I'd be embarrassed about not being as good as them."

Kathy listened to her friends and brother talk together, and she smiled. For the first time since kindergarten she saw Duke as a friend, not just a stranger who was her brother. Her friends were enjoying talking with him too. Love for her friends flooded her. They didn't hate her for how she'd felt toward Megan.

But what would Dad say when she told him?

The thought sent a shiver down her spine.

9

Lee Malcomb

Kathy glanced over her shoulder. Was that jogger following them? She wanted to ask Duke, but he was several paces back talking with Roxie about carving. Megan was chattering to Chelsea and Hannah just ahead of Kathy. They were all going to Betina Quinn's house to work. Duke had said to take the street route instead of going through the park and the path in the woods. Kathy knew he was afraid Cole would be in the park. He'd told the girls about Cole, and they'd said they weren't afraid. Just as Kathy glanced at the jogger again he turned into a long driveway, and Kathy breathed a sigh of relief.

Tall maples lined both sides of the street. The homes all sat far back from the street behind privacy fences or brick walls. Kathy tried to catch a glimpse of the homes, but couldn't. How would it feel to live in such privacy? On Kennedy Street where she lived the homes were quite close together and right in plain view of the street. They only had privacy when they stayed inside and closed the blinds. She knew it was almost the same in The Ravines where the other Best Friends lived.

Just then a rusted-out yellow car stopped across the street, and a man jumped out. It was Cole! Kathy's heart dropped to her feet. She looked back at Duke and saw the fear on his face.

"Run!" shouted Duke.

Chelsea and Hannah grabbed Megan's hands and began running down the street toward the entrance to the Quinn estate. Megan's feet never touched the sidewalk. She swung between the girls like a rag doll.

Blood roared in Kathy's ears as she sped after the girls. She knew Duke and Roxie were right behind her.

"Stop!" shouted Cole. "I just want to talk!"

"Run faster!" Duke yelled.

Suddenly Roxie screamed. Kathy spun around to see Cole struggling with Roxie. Duke swung at Cole, but missed. Kathy ran to help. She clawed at Cole's arm just as Hannah struck him with her fist.

A car screeched to a stop beside them, and a man leaped out. He wore a light gray business suit and shiny black shoes. He was about the same age as Kathy's dad. "Do you kids need help?"

"Yes!" cried Kathy, pointing a shaky finger at Cole. "He's trying to hurt us!"

The stranger caught Cole's arm and twisted it up behind his back. When Cole cried out and released Roxie, she fell forward with a cry. Kathy caught her and held her up. Fear pricked Kathy's skin, and her legs almost gave way. She locked her knees to keep from falling.

"You'll be sorry for this," roared Cole, his face dark with anger.

Kathy shivered as she huddled closer to the others.

"Not as sorry as you," snapped the man. He looked at Duke. "I have a car phone. Call the police and tell them to come pick this man up."

Cole made a sudden move and twisted free. He pushed the stranger against Duke, and they both tumbled to the grass next to the sidewalk. Cole raced to his car, his long greasy hair whipping against his back. He roared away before anyone could stop him.

The man stood up with a groan and helped Duke up. "I'll report this so the police can be on the lookout for him."

"His name is Cole Vangaar," Duke said, trembling.

"Just what was he after?" asked the man, brushing himself off as he hurried toward his car.

"Us," said Duke, running along beside the man. "We know he deals drugs, and he doesn't want us to tell the police."

"I'm glad I stopped." The man slid into his car and picked up his phone.

"Let's go," whispered Kathy.

Duke waved good-bye to the man, and the man waved to them.

"That was terrible," whispered Roxie as they walked away.

"He was an angel," Megan said, looking back. "God sent him to protect us. I saw his wings."

Kathy rolled her eyes, while the others chuckled.

"It was like a nightmare," Hannah said shivering.

"But we're safe," Chelsea added softly.

Kathy nodded and whispered, "Yes, we are." Pictures of what might have happened flashed across her mind, and she groaned.

At the Quinn estate Betina was waiting for them near the gate. She wore a clean white blouse and blue shorts. "I was afraid you'd forgotten to come," she said, holding her hand out to Megan.

"We came," Megan said. "Where's Natalie?"

"On the back porch."

Kathy frowned, but didn't say anything as they followed Betina and Megan down the long drive and around the large house. The problem with Natalie seemed small compared to what they'd just gone through.

Betina stopped near the swing and waited until

the girls and Duke were on the porch. "I ordered a basket of fruit for you. Take something now if you want. There'll be enough for you later during your break too. You may eat while I assign your work to you." She didn't sound like the same person they'd met a few days ago. She sounded like a boss. She smiled down at Megan. "What fruit would you like? Help yourself."

Megan looked the fruit over. The woven basket was almost as big around as the round mahogany table it sat on, and it held enough fruit to feed several families. Smells of apples and oranges were the strongest. Megan finally chose a yellow delicious apple and a bunch of red seedless grapes. "Natalie wants the grapes," Megan said as she climbed onto the swing.

Kathy felt awkward as she looked over the fruit. Sometimes the people they worked for gave them a cookie or a cracker, but no one had ever offered them a giant basket of fruit. She wanted to take an orange, but she didn't know what to do with the peelings, so she took a pear. She waited until the others had their fruit. Chelsea took a banana, Duke an orange, Roxie a bunch of grapes, and Hannah a nectarine. Kathy bit into the pear. It was almost as hard as an apple and tasted delicious. She didn't like it when pears got soft and mushy. Juice trickled down her chin, and she wiped it away with the back of her hand.

Betina pulled a paper from the pocket of her shorts. "I wrote down the first jobs I want done. I hope I have all your names correct. Duke, you mow the lawn, just as you said you would. You'll find the mowers and other lawn tools in the brick building over there." Betina pointed to her left. A wide brick path led to a brick building among a few small trees. "And, Chelsea, you offered to take care of the flowers. The tools are in the same building." Betina looked down at her paper. "Roxie, Kathy, and Hannah, I want you to work together. Start in the first room here." Betina pointed toward the French doors. "The cleaning supplies and vacuum are in a closet just off the kitchen. If any of you need anything, I'll be right here with Megan."

"And Natalie," Megan said around a bite of apple.

Kathy led the way to the kitchen. "I wonder if there's a garbage disposal." She looked under the sink, saw there was, and dropped the pear core in. She ran water in and turned on the disposal. It growled. She clicked it off, then washed and dried her hands.

Roxie opened three doors before she found the closet full of cleaning supplies. "Here it is," she said, stepping inside.

Kathy picked up a can of polish and sneezed as dust floated around. She turned to Hannah and

Roxie and giggled. "I never thought about cleaning a cleaning supplies closet."

Roxie and Hannah giggled as they looked over the shelves of supplies.

"Oh my," Roxie said as she suddenly sank to the floor, her face white.

"What's wrong?" asked Kathy in alarm, kneeling beside her.

"I guess I was still shaking inside from Cole grabbing me," Roxie said, rubbing her arm. "I was so scared!"

Hannah patted Roxie's shoulder. "I'm glad that man came along. It would be funny if he really was an angel, wouldn't it? I've read about things like that."

"Me too," Kathy said. "But I don't think he was an angel. He had a car phone."

Roxie giggled. "I guess an angel wouldn't need a car phone."

"I wish we would've asked him his name," Hannah said. "I know my mom and dad will ask me who it was."

"We didn't thank him either," Kathy said, frowning. "I wish we would've remembered to thank him."

"Maybe we'll see him again," Hannah said.

Roxie slowly stood. "I think I'm all right now."

"Are you sure?" Hannah and Kathy asked together, then giggled.

"I'm sure. Let's get that room cleaned. It shouldn't be very hard to do. I wish we had a giant dust magnet we could pass over the whole house. It would suck up all the dust, and the house would be perfect."

Kathy laughed as she pictured that happening.

Hannah pushed the vacuum cleaner into the room and plugged it in.

Kathy sprayed the special spray onto the leaves of all the plants and soon had them shiny again. She watered them and broke off all the dead leaves. As she dusted the big-screen TV she thought of Dad being on Channel 15. They were taping the shows the next few days that would be aired in three weeks. She wondered if Betina would let all of them watch the show on her TV. Then Kathy remembered Chelsea had a big-screen TV in her special rec room in their basement. She'd let them watch Dad on that. How would it feel to see Dad on TV? She smiled with pride just thinking about it.

"Girls!" hissed Roxie. "Come here!" She frantically motioned to them.

Kathy and Hannah ran across the room to Roxie. "What is it?" asked Kathy.

Roxie held out a photo in a wooden frame. "Look!"

Kathy looked at the photo of a man. It was the man who'd saved them from Cole! "I wonder who he is."

"Let's ask Betina when we finish in here," Hannah said.

They worked quickly, the roar of the vacuum making it impossible to talk.

Later they put away their cleaning supplies and drank cold water.

"It's really funny that Betina has a picture of the man who rescued us," Hannah said.

"Don't make a mystery out of it," Roxie teased, laughing.

Kathy felt strange asking Betina about the man, but she followed the girls to the porch. In the distance she heard the roar of the lawn mower. She saw Chelsea on her hands and knees working on a flower bed.

Roxie turned the photo so Betina could see it. "Who is this man?" Roxie asked.

Megan squealed, "That's our angel! I told you, Betina! And there he is!"

Betina trembled. "He's a fine man, Megan, but he's not an angel. He's Lee Malcomb."

Kathy gasped. "My dad knows him!"

"Now we can thank him for saving us," Hannah said.

Kathy wrinkled her forehead in thought as she tried to remember what else Dad had said. At last she remembered. "Dad says Lee Malcomb has been praying for you, Betina."

Betina's eyes flashed. "He can just stop praying! I don't want him even thinking about me!"

"Why?" asked Megan, leaning her head on Betina's arm. "He's our angel."

"He's to blame for the quarrel Jason and I had before the accident." Betina burst into tears. "And I'll never forgive him! Never!"

Kathy shook her head. She wanted to tell Betina Jesus wanted her to forgive Lee Malcomb, but she could see Betina was too upset to listen.

Megan rubbed Betina's tears with a tissue. "Don't cry. Jesus loves you. Don't cry."

Kathy stepped closer to Hannah and Roxie. "Now we know how to pray for her," whispered Kathy. "We'll pray she comes to forgive Lee Malcomb."

"And that she'll forgive herself too," Roxie said. "I know how hard that can be!"

A few minutes later Duke and Chelsea joined them on the porch. Kathy could tell that the others were as tired as she was. But Megan looked happy and full of energy.

"We'll be back the same time tomorrow," Chelsea said, wiping sweat off her forehead.

Just then Kathy heard someone behind her. She glanced around, and her eyes widened in surprise. It was Lee Malcomb! He'd changed into black pants and a light blue shirt with the cuffs rolled up past his gold watch. His light brown hair was combed back neatly off his forehead. Kathy nudged Roxie, and she in turn nudged Hannah. They all stepped aside to give Lee a full view of Betina standing beside the basket of fruit.

"Hello, Betina," Lee said softly.

"Lee!"

"Our angel!" cried Megan, running to him.

Lee smiled down at Megan, then walked toward Betina. "I'd like to talk to you."

"No! Never!" Betina's eyes flashed with fire. She pointed a shaky finger at him. "Get off my property now!"

"Don't make him leave!" cried Megan, catching Lee's hand in hers. "He's our angel!"

"Megan," Duke said sharply, "come here."

She shook her head and clung tighter to Lee. "I don't want him to leave. Please, Betina."

Betina turned her back on Megan. "Get out! All of you!"

Megan burst into tears. She ran to Kathy and pressed her face against her sister's waist.

Kathy patted Megan's back to soothe her as Lee tried to convince Betina to give him a few minutes of her time.

Betina spun around, picked up an apple, and threw it at Lee. "Get out!"

Lee easily caught the apple. "You can't keep your anger forever, Betina. You know that. Jason wouldn't want that."

"Don't even speak his name!"

A muscle jumped in Lee's jaw. Pain filled his brown eyes. He held the apple out to Duke, who stood the closest to him. "Put it back in the basket and I'll give you kids a ride home."

"Thanks," Duke mumbled.

Kathy breathed a sigh of relief. She'd dreaded the walk home. "Did you tell the police about Cole?" she asked.

Lee nodded. "They were already looking for him. It gives them a reason to look harder."

Duke put the apple in the basket. "We'll be back tomorrow, Betina," he said gently.

She nodded, but didn't take her eyes off Lee.

"And I'll be back," Lee said firmly.

Betina lifted her chin, but didn't say a word.

Kathy took Megan's hand and followed the others off the porch. At the corner of the house Kathy looked back. Betina stood where they'd left her, a sad, faraway look on her face. Tears burned Kathy's eyes as she silently prayed for Betina Quinn.

10

Natalie

Kathy smoothed the emerald-green and cream bedspread even though it was already smooth. She touched the emerald-green throw pillows and the paisley pillow next to them. She picked up the rag doll Grandma had made for her when she was three years old and hugged her close. Dad had said he'd call her when he finished talking on the phone to Lee Malcomb. Kathy moaned. She'd have to tell him the terrible thing she'd said about Megan. It didn't matter that the other girls had felt the same about their little brothers and sisters; it was still wrong. Dad would get upset with her and maybe yell at her. She whimpered and dropped the doll on her bed. She deserved to be yelled at! She even deserved to be spanked—and she hadn't been spanked since she was eight!

Her door opened, and her heart dropped to her

feet. Megan poked her head in, and Kathy sighed in relief.

"Kathy, will you read to me?"

"Not now. I'm waiting for Dad to call me."

"But I can't go to sleep." Megan twisted her pink and white nightgown around her hand, tightening it around her thin body. "Read me just one story. Please. Please?"

"Oh, all right!" Kathy pushed past Megan and stalked next door to Megan's room. The room was decorated in three shades of pink. Kathy sometimes wondered if Megan ever got tired of pink.

"Here!" Megan thrust the book *Nothing Sticks Like a Shadow* into Kathy's hand.

"You already know this by heart," Kathy said impatiently.

"I don't care! Read it again. Please. Please?"

With a long sigh Kathy sat on the edge of Megan's bed and opened the book. "You have to lie down first."

Megan plopped down on her pillow and put her hands behind her head.

In an impatient voice Kathy started the story about Rabbit and Woodchuck. Soon she got involved in it and had fun reading it. She peeked at Megan. Her eyes were closed, and she looked asleep. Carefully Kathy put the book on the shelf beside the bed. She tiptoed from the room and almost ran into Dad. Butterflies fluttered wildly in her stomach.

"I came to tell you I have to go out," Dad said, slipping his arm around Kathy. "But tomorrow we'll talk. I won't forget."

"It doesn't matter," Kathy said, trying not to sound as relieved as she felt. "I'm all right now."

Dad smiled and kissed her cheek. "Tomorrow," he said firmly.

She nodded. She bit her lip as he strode down the hall away from her. Just as she started back to her room Megan called her. Frowning she stepped back into Megan's room. "I thought you were asleep."

"I can't sleep without Natalie."

"Megan!"

"I forgot her at Betina's house." Megan slid out of bed and caught Kathy's hand. "Can we go get her right now?"

"No! You know Mom wouldn't let us do that. It's almost dark out."

Megan's face puckered up. "I want Natalie!"

Kathy picked up Megan and dropped her on the bed. "Go to sleep! I don't want to talk to you any longer! Stay in bed or I'll tell Mom you're still awake."

Megan buried her face in her pillow and began sobbing.

Kathy ran to her room and closed the door with a snap.

Someone knocked, and she jumped.

"It's me," Duke said.

Kathy opened the door and frowned.

"I'm going to make a banana milk shake. Want one?"

"Yes!" Kathy laughed in relief as she stepped into the hallway. The smell of Megan's bubble bath still hung in the air. "I was afraid you were going to say something mean. I'm not used to you being nice to me."

Duke flushed as they walked down the carpeted hall. "And I thought you were the one being mean to me."

Kathy stopped in surprise. "Me mean? I never said or did anything to you!"

"You ignored me like I was nothing!"

"But I thought that's what you wanted."

Duke shrugged. "I'd rather be friends, wouldn't you?"

"Yes!"

"Me too," Megan said, jumping out at them with a giggle.

"Get to bed!" Kathy and Duke both cried at once. They looked at each other and laughed.

Megan burst into tears. "You hate me. Everybody hates me!"

"Go to bed right now," Kathy said sharply.

"I want Natalie!"

"She's not here," snapped Duke. Then he flushed scarlet. "You make even me forget she's not real! She's only in your head." He tapped Megan's head.

Megan cried harder.

"What's going on?" asked Mom as she started down the hall from the living room. "Megan, why aren't you in bed?"

Megan ran to Mom and flung herself against her. "I want Natalie!"

Kathy and Duke looked at each other and walked to the kitchen. They were glad to let Mom deal with Megan.

"She's such a baby," Duke said as he got out the blender.

"Well, she is only four," Kathy said. "But she is a baby!" Kathy peeled two ripe bananas and laid them on the counter.

Duke dropped several ice cubes into the blender and ground them into fine chips. Next he added a cup of milk, a big scoop of vanilla ice cream, a teaspoon of sugar, and the bananas. He put the lid on the blender and pushed the grind button, let it up, then pushed it again. The noise filled the quiet room.

Kathy set out two tall glasses. She watched Duke fill them, then took a long drink of hers. It was cold and delicious. Slowly she walked to the table and sat down. It felt strange sharing a banana shake with Duke.

He sat across from her, a thoughtful expression on his face as he drank. He set down his glass and wiped his mouth with a white paper napkin. "I wonder what Lee Malcomb talked to Dad about."

"Betina probably."

"I heard Dad ask him about two kids."

Kathy shrugged as she took another long drink. "I never heard anything about the two kids. Was Betina's lawn hard to mow?"

"It would've been, but she has a riding lawn mower with a bag hooked on it to catch the clippings. Otherwise I would've had to rake. I hate raking!"

"Me too." Kathy leaned forward. "Isn't it strange that she kept the photo of Lee Malcomb?"

Duke nodded.

Before he could say anything Mom walked in and sat down with a long, tired sigh. Dark rings circled her eyes. She wore a flowered blouse over tan shorts. "This Natalie business has me tired right out."

"Why don't you just tell her Natalie is make-believe?" asked Duke impatiently.

"I have." Mom pushed her short hair back. "I've prayed about it too. I know God knows what to do. Now I need Him to tell me."

Kathy held out her glass. "Want a drink of my shake?"

Mom took it and drank a little, then handed it back. "Thanks," she said smiling.

"We were talking about Betina Quinn and Lee Malcomb," Kathy said. "Do you know anything about them?"

"I know they were sweethearts in college before Betina met Jason Quinn and married him."

Duke told Mom about Lee's visit to the estate. "She was sure mean to him."

"Holding a grudge does a lot of damage," Mom said. "You two remember that. Never hold grudges, and never stay angry. Jesus wants us to love like He does."

Kathy ducked her head. Jesus would never say He wished Megan was dead!

Mom talked a while longer about loving each other, then said, "I want you two to be patient with Megan while we sort out this Natalie thing. Will you?"

"Yes," Kathy said, ready to promise anything that would make her feel better.

"I'll try," Duke said. "But it's hard. I can't understand how she can think Natalie's real."

Mom sat up straight and laughed right out loud. "I have it! I know what to do. We have to carefully show Megan Natalie is make-believe. Here's what we'll do."

Kathy listened as Mom told them to play along with Megan, then say, "I really had a good time with you and Natalie. She's a fun make-believe friend."

"It won't be easy, but I'll do it," Duke said.

"Using your imagination isn't wrong," Mom said. "But it's very important to know the difference between make-believe and reality."

Kathy nodded. She wished her problem could be solved as easily as the Natalie problem.

The next day Kathy thankfully worked at the Crandall house, ran an errand for old Mrs. Lemford, then went home to clean her room. After Megan's nap they met the Best Friends and walked to the Quinn estate. Dad had told them a policeman was cruising the area, so it would be safe to walk.

"Today I'm taking Natalie home," Megan said firmly as they walked around Betina's house to the back porch.

Kathy and Duke exchanged looks, but didn't say anything as they followed the others to where Betina waited near another large basket of fruit. She wore jeans and a yellow pullover shirt. Her hair hung in a single braid down her back.

"I had almost decided not to have you back because of Lee Malcomb," Betina said with a catch in her voice. "I don't want anyone to ask about him or talk about him to me. If he comes here again, you'll have to leave and never return."

"Are you mad at us?" Megan asked as she looked up at Betina.

"Not you, sweetie." Betina bent down and kissed Megan, then faced the others. "Are you sure you want to continue working for me?"

"Yes," they said in subdued voices.

"Good. Duke, continue mowing. Chelsea, you still work on the flower beds. Would you like help with them?"

Chelsea nodded. "There are more than I thought."

"Who would like to help her?"

Kathy looked at Roxie and Hannah. They shrugged.

"Hannah, you help her," Betina said. "Roxie and Kathy, work in the den today. It's to the left of the room you did yesterday. If you finish there, go to the next room. You know where the supplies are."

Kathy and Roxie walked quietly through the house to the supply closet.

Roxie leaned against a shelf and looked at Kathy. "Don't you ever get tired of working?"

"Yes. Do you?"

Roxie nodded. "Last summer I went swimming a lot. And I hung out at the mall. But so far this summer all I've done is work!"

"You did go on vacation at that ranch in Wyoming."

"Yes." Roxie smiled dreamily. "It was so much fun! I want to go again next year. The whole family had a great time. Even Grandma."

As they worked Roxie told about her grandma learning to ride a horse.

The den took less time than they thought it would, so they moved to the next room.

Kathy looked at the large oak desk, the walls lined with books, and the leather furniture. Sunlight filtered through the dusty windows and sliding glass door. "This must've been Jason Quinn's study."

"It's huge! And over all that dust I can smell the leather." Roxie ran a finger over the soft black leather chair. "It smells just like a saddle."

"My mom would love a study like this," Kathy said as she started dusting. She picked a book up off the desk, and it fell from her fingers to the floor. "Ooops. I don't think I damaged it." She picked it up, and a paper fluttered from it to the floor.

Roxie scooped up the paper and unfolded it. "It's a note from Jason to Lee."

"Don't read it," Kathy whispered in alarm.

Roxie jumped away from Kathy and read, "'Lee, please take care of Mark and Allie for me until I can convince Betina to take them in. I know she will change her mind, but right now she doesn't want any child but Carlene. You're a good friend to both of us. God's best to you. Jason.'"

Kathy grabbed the note, folded it and stuck it back in the book. "You should not have read that!"

"I wonder who Mark and Allie are?"

With a cry Betina ran across the room and pulled the note from the book. She read it, then burst into wild tears.

Kathy and Roxie looked helplessly at each other. "I don't know what to do," whispered Kathy.

Betina held the note close to herself and ran back out of the room.

Kathy sank weakly down on the nearest chair. "She'll kick us out for sure now."

Roxie leaned back against the desk, her face white. "I shouldn't have read it, I know, but sometimes my curiosity goes crazy."

"Let's just keep working until she tells us to quit." Kathy slowly cleared off the desk and polished it to a shine.

Later they walked outdoors where the others were already waiting to go home. Betina didn't say a word about the note. Her eyes looked full of pain, but she smiled as she thanked them for doing their jobs well.

"We'll be back tomorrow," Duke said.

"I have to take Natalie home with me," Megan announced.

Betina hugged Megan. "All right. You were kind to share her with me."

Duke turned away, his face red.

Kathy held out her hand to Megan. "Let's go."

"See you tomorrow," Chelsea said.

"Bye," Hannah and Roxie added with a wave.

"Come on, Natalie," Megan said as she walked off the porch with Kathy. "You got to walk faster than that or we'll never get home."

Kathy bit back a groan. Should she try what Mom had suggested? After a minute of thought she decided she'd try. "Megan, Natalie is just a little girl, you know. She can't walk as fast as the rest of us." She hoped her friends or Duke couldn't hear her.

"That's right," Megan said, slowing down so much that they fell behind the others by several steps.

"What are you going to do with Natalie now that you have her back?" Kathy wanted to scream at Megan that Natalie wasn't real, but she bit the words back.

"How come you're nice to Natalie now?" Megan asked as she tilted her head back to look up at Kathy.

"Mom said to."

"Oh. Well, Natalie is sure glad. She got tired of you being mean to her."

"Sorry, Natalie. I won't be mean again. Want to play dolls when we get home?"

Megan giggled and bounced up and down. "She does! And I do too!"

All the way down the street Kathy forced herself to keep up the talk. Finally she said, "You have good times with Natalie, Megan. She's a fun make-believe friend."

"She's my very best friend," Megan said, sounding very pleased.

Kathy glanced at *her* best friends walking and talking with Duke. She wanted to run to catch up to them, but she stayed with Megan, holding her hand and swinging it back and forth.

11

The Picnic

Kathy walked listlessly to the kitchen for breakfast. She'd stayed awake a long time last night waiting to see if Dad would talk to her. He'd finally stopped in to apologize. He'd had to work overtime at the studio, then Lee Malcomb had needed his help. Kathy hadn't minded a bit.

In the kitchen she leaned against the counter, trying to decide if she wanted cornflakes or raisin bran. She heard the family already at the table, but she was still too sleepy to look at them.

"We have a surprise for you, Kit Kat," Dad said.

Kathy turned slowly. "What is it?" she asked without interest.

"We've talked to the McCreas, the Shigwams, and the Shoulders," Mom said. "And we all agreed that you girls have been working too hard. You're taking today off, and we're all going to the park for a picnic."

"But I have to help at the Crandall house," Kathy said.

"Roxie's dad is going to water the animals," Dad said. "The other work can wait."

A weight seemed to lift off Kathy, and she laughed breathlessly. She hadn't realized how tired she was from working every day. She sank to her chair with a loud sigh of relief. "I don't know how you go to work every day—and you've been doing it for years!" she said to Mom and Dad. "I don't think I want to be a grown-up."

"I'm glad you can be a child a while longer," Dad said, grinning. "You're eleven years old, so enjoy it while you can." He turned to Duke. "And you too, Duke. Have fun today, and don't think about the troubles you've had lately or the hard work you've done for Betina Quinn."

Kathy remembered the note Roxie had read in Jason Quinn's study. "Dad, what do you know about two kids . . . Mark and Allie?"

Dad lifted his brows in surprise. "Did Betina mention them?"

"No." Kathy told him about the note and Betina's reaction.

"Well, well." Dad stabbed his fingers through his blond waves. "Mark and Allie were the kids Jason wanted them to adopt. He was their godfather, so when their parents died in a plane crash, he was in charge of them. Betina refused to take them in. They're staying with Lee now. He offered to take them since he's known them since birth. He didn't want them put in foster care. Mark is five and Allie four."

"My age!" cried Megan. "She can be my friend!"

"She'd be a real friend," Mom said, patting Megan's hand, "and even more fun to play with than your make-believe friend Natalie."

"Right." Dad smiled and nodded at Megan, then turned back to Kathy and Duke. "Now Lee doesn't know if he wants to part with them, but he's single. He has a housekeeper taking care of them while he's at work. He wants Betina to come into the picture. He knows she needs somebody, and he'd like it to be him and the kids—he'd like to marry her."

"How romantic," Mom said, smiling dreamily.

Kathy thought so too. She couldn't wait to see the Best Friends and tell them the wonderful story. Maybe they'd find a way to get Betina and Lee together.

An hour later Kathy carried a cooler full of punch to the picnic tables the McCreas had saved for all of them.

"Kathy," Duke called softly behind her.

She turned and waited for him. He was carrying a bag full of food. He looked worried. "What's wrong?" she asked sharply.

"What if Cole is here today?"

Kathy gasped. "I hadn't thought about that!"

"We'll have to watch for him. Don't go off by yourself, and don't let Megan out of your sight."

Kathy nodded grimly. Suddenly the beautiful day was marred by possible danger from Cole Vangaar. "Are you sure he's not in jail?"

"He's not. I asked Dad. He said police are cruising the park area and that we don't have to worry, but we still need to be careful." Duke shifted the bag. "Let's put these things down, then find the others. Roxie said she might bring something she started to carve."

"Oh, I hope so!" Kathy walked beside Duke to the table and set the cooler down. She said hello to Glenn and Billie McCrea. She saw Mike doing flips and tumbles in the grass while the Best Friends watched. Kathy ran to join them. She wished she was as good in gymnastics as Mike. When he finished his routine, everyone clapped and he bowed low, then ran to the tall slide.

Rob McCrea asked Duke if he'd like to play a game of tennis. He agreed, and they ran to an empty court.

Kathy turned to Chelsea, Roxie, and Hannah. "Doesn't it feel good to be together just to play?" she asked with a giggle.

"Yes!" they said together.

They walked to the shade of a tall oak and sat in the lush grass. Kathy told them what her dad had said about Lee and Betina and the two kids.

"She's too angry to ever let them even come near her," Roxie said.

"But she can change." Chelsea touched her *I'm A Best Friend* button. "I changed."

"Me too," Roxie whispered.

"Now we have to find a way to help Betina and Lee," Hannah said. Then her face clouded over. "But I don't know if I can do much to help. We have a family reunion on the 4th of July, and I have to get my special dress ready."

"We'll help you," Kathy said. Hannah had told her about the Ottawa Indian clothes she was going to wear. She still had to make the special necklaces. They had to be just right, according to her dad.

Chelsea rocked back and forth. "Oh, I wish I'd never made those long-distance phone calls to Sid! I can't do anything I want when I want because I'm always working. I hate it! I'll be glad when school starts so I can give up my jobs!" Then she shivered. "Then again, I don't know if I want school to start . . . A new school and all new kids and teachers."

"We'll be there," Hannah said.

"And that'll help," Chelsea agreed.

"Guess what I decided to do?" Roxie said in a low voice.

"Quit school?" asked Chelsea with a giggle.

Roxie shook her head.

"Carve an animal," Kathy said, grinning.

"Duke told you!" cried Roxie. "I wanted to surprise all of you." She opened the pouch hooked around her waist. "Look . . . You can't tell yet what it is, but I can."

Kathy leaned forward and studied the piece of half-carved wood. She wasn't sure what it was, but she liked the delicate lines Roxie had already carved.

"It's a squirrel," Roxie said softly. "It's just like Grandpa always told me. I saw this piece of wood and I saw a squirrel in it. It made me shiver all over."

They looked at it and talked about it for a while. Then Roxie put it back in her pouch.

Kathy glanced up, then froze. Had she seen Cole peering at her from around a tree? Maybe it was her imagination. The color drained from her face, and she moved restlessly. The grass tickled her bare legs.

"What's wrong, Kathy?" whispered Hannah.

"I think I saw Cole," Kathy blurted out.

"Let's go get him!" cried Roxie, leaping up.

Kathy pulled Roxie back down. "He's dangerous. And maybe he isn't even there. We'd hate to tackle a stranger."

"That would be embarrassing," Chelsea said with a laugh.

"Why don't we walk over that way? If it is Cole, we'll run and tell our dads," Hannah said.

Kathy nodded, and the others agreed. Slowly they walked together, making sure they talked together as naturally as they could. Kids played at the slides, swings, and the merry-go-round. A Frisbee flew past the girls, and a spotted dog leaped and caught it, then took it back to the teenage boy who'd tossed it.

Kathy's heart thundered as she casually glanced over where she'd seen the man she thought was Cole. It was Cole! His back was to her, and he was talking to Brody. Kathy gripped Hannah's wrist. "It's Cole," she whispered. "Let's turn slowly and go tell our dads. But don't run. He might suspect something."

The girls kept talking the best they could as they turned and walked toward their families. The picnic tables seemed about fifty miles away. Sweat soaked Kathy's curls and made them curl even tighter. She glanced toward the tennis court just as Duke looked her way. She lifted her hand to him. He waved back, but kept on playing. She'd hoped he'd know she wanted him.

She felt out of breath when she reached Dad, even though she'd walked and hadn't run at all. She caught his arm, and he stopped talking right in the middle of a sentence.

"What's frightened you so much?" Dad asked in concern.

The other girls stood by their fathers as they asked the same thing.

Kathy quickly told about seeing Cole.

"You girls stay right here," Kathy's dad said. "Men, let's go."

"Call 911, Billie," Chelsea's dad told her mom.

"I'll go with you," Kathy's mom said as Billie jumped up.

The girls sank down on the bench so they could watch their dads go after Cole. The men walked toward the wishing well so Cole wouldn't know they were after him, then ducked behind a clump of bushes. Kathy held her breath as she lost sight of them. She knew they were running behind the bushes toward the spot where she'd seen Cole. Suddenly Cole ran into sight. The men raced after him, spreading out. Kathy's dad tackled him and sent him sprawling to the ground. The men quickly bound him with their belts and propped him against a tree to wait for the police.

Kathy breathed a sigh of relief. She wanted to shout for joy, but she was shaking too badly.

"They got him," whispered Roxie, shivering as she moved closer to Kathy.

Within a few minutes the police arrived and took Cole away in their car.

Kathy jumped up and ran to Dad, hugging him tightly. "You were so brave!"

"I was, wasn't I?" Dad chuckled.

She looked up and saw that he'd been afraid. That surprised her. She'd thought he wasn't afraid of anything.

He gently pushed her away as he looked across the park. "I see Brody. I want to speak to that young man."

Kathy watched Dad stride toward Brody. Duke joined him. To her surprise Brody didn't run away. Dad slipped an arm around Brody's thin shoulder and talked to him. Finally he walked him toward the picnic tables.

Tears stung Kathy's eyes as she realized Dad planned to invite Brody to spend the day with all of them. Silently she prayed they'd be able to help Brody.

Several minutes later they all sat around the picnic tables with their plates loaded with food. Hannah's dad asked the blessing on the food, and everyone said, "Amen."

Kathy picked up her hamburger and bit into it. Catsup dribbled down her chin, but she didn't care. This was a beautiful day. It was perfect! Then she thought of the small black spot in her heart. Would it be there forever?

12

Unsettled

Kathy sat beside Mom on the couch watching TV. Megan was already asleep for the night. Kathy listened for the sound of the back door opening. Dad and Duke had taken Brody home so they could talk to his mother. Kathy hugged a throw pillow tightly to her. She couldn't wait to hear what happened.

Just as a commercial came on TV the back door opened and Kathy sped to the kitchen. Dad and Duke were laughing as they walked in. "Tell me everything!" cried Kathy.

"We want to hear it all," Mom said from behind Kathy.

Kathy glanced back in surprise. She hadn't known Mom was even interested.

Dad opened the refrigerator and pulled out the pitcher of punch. "Anyone want a drink?" he asked as he filled a glass.

"I do," Duke said, setting a glass beside Dad's.

Kathy set a glass beside Duke's. Dad filled it, and she took a sip as she walked to the table. Every second seemed like an hour.

Dad drank half his punch, then set the glass on the table and leaned back in his chair with his hands locked behind his head. "Mrs. Vangaar was very upset, naturally, over Cole's arrest."

"What about Mr. Vangaar?" asked Mom sharply.

"He walked out on them about five years ago," Duke said. "Brody was too embarrassed to tell me. I always thought his dad was away a lot on business."

"We talked to Mrs. Vangaar about us helping Brody." Dad sighed heavily. "Every child needs a father. Especially Brody since his big brother took the route he took. Anyway, Mrs. Vangaar was thankful we even offered to help. We're going to take Brody to church every Sunday with us. Mrs. Vangaar works on Sundays, and if she doesn't she'll lose her job."

"He's going to youth group with us too," Duke said.

Kathy could tell Duke was excited about having Brody around so much. Would it make a difference in Duke?

"I told Brody that he and Duke can practice guitar at our house, so that means Brody will be spending a lot of time here. I didn't think you'd mind, Grace."

"I don't, Tommy. But, Kathy, what about you? Does it bother you?"

It did a little, but what could she say? "It's all right," she said with a slight shrug.

"We're going to be his extended family," Dad said, reaching for his glass.

"Tell them what else, Dad," Duke said with a chuckle.

Dad finished his punch and set his glass down. He grinned and rubbed his hand over his hair. "Well, Brody said he's going to get his hair cut since I did. He wants to look like me."

"That's sweet," Mom said.

Dad pushed his chair back and stretched and yawned. "He's good on guitar. With a little help he'll make an outstanding musician."

Kathy glanced at Duke. He was beaming with pride. She was glad he wasn't jealous. She could see Duke was happy about finally having another boy in the family. Suddenly Kathy realized that with Brody around so much Duke wouldn't have time to watch Megan. Kathy's heart sank. She had planned to talk to him about it now that they'd become friends. She fingered her glass as the others continued talking about Brody. Just how would having Brody here affect her friendship with Duke? Would he ignore her again like he had in the past? Would he expect her to ignore him?

"Is there a problem, Kit Kat?"

Kathy flushed at Dad's question.

"Out with it," Dad said.

Kathy moved restlessly. "I won't know how to act around Brody." Oh, why couldn't she say what she really meant?

"Treat him like you do Duke," Mom said. "You're a kind, sweet girl. Continue to be that."

Kathy nodded, her heart sinking. If they only knew how terrible she really was!

"Remember to add Brody to your prayer list," Dad said. "He needs to know Jesus as his Savior." Dad leaned forward. "I want to keep Brody from following in Cole's footsteps. You kids can help by loving him and letting him share your life."

"We could take him to the Quinn estate to work with us," Duke said.

"He's not a *King's Kid*," Megan said sharply.

"He can help anyway," Dad said. "It'll do him good. He's on his own too much, with nothing to do."

"He can help me finish Betina's yard," Duke said, nodding. "There's a lot to do. It would take me a long time on my own."

Kathy knew it wouldn't do any good to argue. Brody would go with them.

She thought about Brody again the next day as

she pedaled her bike up to her garage. She'd just returned from helping at the Crandall house. The kittens had looked bigger after not seeing them for two days. She'd told the girls about taking Brody in, and they'd been excited. They'd also told her she'd get used to having him around.

She left her bike beside the garage. Was Brody in the house practicing guitar with Duke?

Just then she glanced toward Mrs. Sobol's house. A curtain moved! Fear pricked her skin. Cole was still in jail, so who was in Mrs. Sobol's house? Could it be Duke? Maybe he'd gone to take care of things now that Dad had said it was safe to take care of the house again.

Her heart in her mouth, Kathy walked slowly toward Mrs. Sobol's house. The curtain moved again, and Kathy caught a glimpse of a man's face. Shivers ran up and down her spine. With a strangled cry she spun around and ran back to her house.

"Mom!" she shouted. There was no answer. She ran to the living room, calling as she ran. Mom wasn't home, and neither was Megan.

"Duke might be home," muttered Kathy as she ran to Dad's music room. She heard guitar music. Relief washed over her. She wasn't alone! She burst through the door. Duke and Brody looked up in surprise. The music stopped abruptly.

"Duke! I saw a man at Mrs. Sobol's!" cried Kathy, breathing hard.

Duke jumped up and set the guitar on the stand as he quickly told Brody about their neighbor lady.

Even in her panic Kathy noticed Brody had his dark hair cut short and was dressed in clean jeans and a blue T-shirt. He looked different than he had in the park.

"We'll take care of it," Brody said gruffly. "I'm stronger than I look."

Duke nodded as they slipped out the French doors. Kathy hesitated, then raced after them. She wasn't going to be left behind for any reason! The hot sun burned down on her. A car with a noisy muffler drove past, making her jump.

Brody stopped, and Kathy bumped into him.

"Go back to the house," Brody whispered harshly.

Kathy bristled. "I will not!"

Duke frowned over his shoulder at Kathy. "Go back. We can take care of this."

Kathy stamped her foot. She suddenly realized that she felt just like Megan probably felt whenever they treated her like a baby. "I'm going with you. I mean it!"

"Oh, all right," Duke said impatiently.

"Don't let her," Brody said. "We don't need her."

Kathy glared at him. "And we don't need you!" She saw the pain in his eyes, and she wanted to grab back the words.

Brody ran from the yard and down the sidewalk away from them.

Kathy wanted to shout for him to come back, but she didn't. She glanced at Duke. Would he be mad at her? He was looking at Mrs. Sobol's house.

"Stay close to me," Duke said as he strode across the yard.

She ran after him, thankful he didn't yell at her for being mean to Brody. They stopped at the back door. Kathy's heart pounded against her rib cage. Duke looked as frightened as she felt.

He knocked on the door.

Kathy moved closer to him, her eyes glued to the door.

Suddenly it opened, and she shrieked.

"What do you kids want?" asked the man inside.

Duke cleared his throat. "Mrs. Sobol asked us to take care of her house while she's gone. Who are you and what are you doing in her house?"

"I'm Adam Sobol."

Kathy gasped. It was Mrs. Sobol's son!

"Aren't you the kids from next door?" asked Adam.

"Yes," they whispered.

Adam smiled. "Don't you recognize me?" He stroked his chin. "Well, maybe not, since I shaved off my beard and mustache."

"But why are you here?" asked Duke.

"I had business in town. I told Mom I'd be here, but she probably forgot."

Kathy sighed in relief. The man really was Adam Sobol! She'd seen him several times, but he'd always had a beard and mustache. "We thought somebody bad had taken the key and was using the house."

"No. Just me," Adam said. "I'll be here another three days, then you can continue taking care of it."

Duke glanced up at the hanging pot. "Did you have a key made?"

"Yes. I thought I'd better have a spare key in case Mom decided to hide the key somewhere else and not tell me." Adam chuckled. "Mom doesn't remember things."

"I'm glad the mystery is solved," Duke said.

"Me too," said Adam. "I kept thinking someone had been in the house, and it made me nervous."

They talked a few more minutes, then Kathy walked home beside Duke. She wanted to say something about Brody, but didn't.

Duke stopped at the garage. "I'll get Brody and try to explain what happened."

Kathy's eyes widened. "I thought you'd be mad at me!"

"I'm not. Brody doesn't know how to handle sisters. He doesn't have one. But I have two." Duke rolled his eyes and grinned. "I guess I've learned a few things about sisters."

"I guess I'm learning a few things about brothers." Kathy smiled. "I was afraid you'd ignore me again with Brody around all the time."

"I'll try not to. But it's hard to remember. You know how it is when you're with *your* best friends. You forget all about me."

Kathy flushed. She'd never thought about that. "I guess I do. But I'll try not to after this."

"Good." Duke smiled, then ran to get his bike. "I'll be back as soon as I can."

"Tell Brody I'm sorry." Kathy was pleased to realize she meant it. "I do want him to come back with you."

"You better tell him yourself," Duke said as he wheeled his bike to the sidewalk. "He might think I made it up."

Kathy bit her lip. "I guess I can tell him."

"I'll help you." Duke grinned at her, then pedaled away.

Kathy laughed under her breath. Duke really was nice even if he was her brother! She watched until he was out of sight.

13

Mark and Allie

Holding Megan's hand, Kathy stood beside her best friends and Duke and Brody. They were about a half-block from the Quinn estate. The large trees sheltered them from the blazing sun. Kathy trembled as she watched Lee Malcomb walk from his car with a boy and a girl on either side of him. They were dark-haired, and both were short and slight.

"She's my size," Megan whispered happily as she looked at Allie.

"Kids, I'd like you to meet Mark and Allie," Lee Malcomb said smiling. "Mark is five, and Allie is four. They're excited about going with you today."

"Betina will be mad," Kathy said just above a whisper.

"She'll be happy once she gets to know Mark and Allie," Lee said.

Kathy heard the quiver in Lee's voice and saw

how nervous he was. Dad had told them this was Lee's last try to get Betina to listen to him with an open mind. Dad had said he wanted all of them to help. They'd voted and agreed 100 percent. Now Kathy wondered if they'd made the right decision. What if Betina yelled at Mark and Allie?

"God is with you," Lee said softly.

Kathy nodded as they all agreed.

Megan stepped up to Allie with her hand out. "I'll take care of you. We can be friends."

Allie took Megan's hand, and they skipped ahead of Kathy toward the Quinn estate. Mark held back until Duke and Brody talked to him. Then he walked between them with his head high.

"I'll be back later," Lee said as he walked to his car.

Kathy trembled as she hurried with her friends to the gate that led into the estate. Her mouth felt bone-dry as they ran around to the back porch. Birds fluttered through the trees. A squirrel scolded, then was quiet. Would Betina scold too and send them away with angry shouts?

Megan and Allie ran up the steps together. "Hi, Betina. This is my friend Allie. I told her you'd like her."

Betina looked down at Allie with a slight frown, then turned to look at Mark.

"They're our friends," Kathy said quickly. "We didn't think you'd care if they came today."

"I suppose not," Betina said uncertainly. She nervously tugged her green T-shirt down over her jeans.

Megan led Allie to the swing. "We can swing while Betina tells us a story. Right, Betina?"

"I . . . I suppose."

"Come on, Mark," Megan said, patting the swing seat. "You can sit here."

Betina licked her lips. "Duke, you and your friend continue with the lawn. Girls, you can all work inside. I did three of the rooms this morning, but there are still more to do. I'll show you."

Kathy walked stiffly into the house. Did Betina realize who Mark and Allie were? She'd read their names in the note. But maybe she thought these were two other kids with the same names.

Betina led them upstairs after they picked up their cleaning supplies. She stopped at her little girl's bedroom, but didn't look inside. "Start here and work your way down the hall," Betina said with a catch in her voice.

The girls walked silently into Carlene's room.

"There's a balcony going out from the bedroom next door. You can shake the dust rags out there," Betina said. She sounded close to tears.

Kathy couldn't look at the toys with Betina in the room. It felt like she'd be looking into Betina's greatest pain.

Betina turned away with her head bent. She stood that way a long time, then finally walked out.

"She's so sad," whispered Chelsea, blinking away tears.

"I think we hurt her by bringing Mark and Allie," Roxie said with a catch in her voice.

"But we did it." Hannah pushed open the windows and let the breeze blow in. "And we can't take back what we did."

Kathy slowly cleaned off the dresser and polished it carefully. She couldn't speak in case she started crying.

"Let's do an extra good job on Carlene's bedroom," Chelsea said, sounding very businesslike. She loaded stuffed animals into a basket. "I'll take these out on the balcony and dust them."

With very little talk the girls cleaned the room. It smelled like lemon polish when they finished. Kathy was pleased at how nice it looked.

With the four of them working together they cleaned three rooms in just a few minutes.

Kathy stood in the doorway of the last bedroom on the right side of the hall. She heard giggling. Her eyes widened, and she muttered, "Oh no!"

She dashed down the hall and stopped at Carlene's door. Megan, Allie, and Mark were playing with the stuffed animals and the toys. All the strength poured from Kathy's body, and she sagged against the door frame.

Megan turned with a laugh. "Kathy, we're having fun."

Kathy took a deep breath and forced herself to stand. "You have to go back outdoors," she whispered hoarsely.

"We like it in here," Allie said.

Kathy rushed forward and put several toys back on the shelves where they'd been. "You can't touch those things! You have to go out right now."

"Oh no!" Betina suddenly cried from the doorway.

Kathy watched the color drain from Betina's face as she stared in horror at the little kids playing with Carlene's things.

Megan and Allie ran to Betina and caught her hands. "Come play with us," Megan said. "You'll have fun."

Tears trickled down Betina's cheeks as she tried to pull away. She didn't seem to have enough strength.

"Let her sit down, Megan," Kathy said softly. She turned the white rocker.

Betina sank into the rocker and leaned her head back while tears continued to fall.

"Please don't cry," Allie said, crawling up on Betina's lap. She rubbed at Betina's cheeks with her hands, then kissed Betina's damp cheeks. "It'll be all right now."

Mark stood on one side of Betina and Megan the other. They patted her shoulders and talked quietly to her.

Kathy crept from the bedroom to leave Betina alone with the kids. Maybe they could do what no one else had been able to do.

"What's going on?" Chelsea whispered.

"We heard voices," Hannah said, and Roxie agreed.

Kathy led them to Carlene's doorway and motioned inside. They peeked in, then quietly walked away.

"I hope her heart's no longer broken," Hannah said, brushing a tear off her dark lash.

"Lee will be coming soon," Roxie said. "I hope she doesn't throw us all out."

"She won't," Kathy whispered. "We've been praying. Remember?"

Several minutes later Kathy heard Duke's voice on the stairs, then Lee's voice. Her stomach knotted. She peeked out the door of the room they were cleaning just as Lee stepped into Carlene's bedroom. Duke ran quietly back downstairs. Kathy motioned to the girls, and they followed her down the hall. They clustered around Carlene's door. Mark and Allie were hugging Lee. Betina still sat in the rocker, and she was staring at Lee. Megan was coloring in a book at a small table and didn't look up.

"Betina, it's way past the time we should have talked," Lee said gently.

Betina bit her lip and nodded. "It wasn't fair for you to send them here today," she whispered.

"I had to do *something.*" Lee knelt beside the rocker and looked imploringly into Betina's face. "They need you . . . I need you."

"Oh, Lee."

"And you need us."

Kathy's heart almost burst. She could see that her friends felt the same. Finally they tiptoed back to the room they'd been cleaning.

"I hope they get married," Hannah said with a loud sigh.

"I hope we get invited to the wedding," Chelsea said.

"Me too," Kathy and Roxie whispered.

Kathy whirled around the room. "I was so frightened when Megan disappeared that day. I never dreamed she'd make such a difference in anyone's life. She's such a hassle, but I love her anyway." And it was true! She did love Megan! Tears welled up in Kathy's eyes, and she brushed them quickly away. Was it possible she really didn't want Megan dead?

14

More Trouble

With a banana in her hand Kathy sank down on the steps beside the Best Friends to wait for the boys to finish the lawn and Megan to come downstairs. Betina, Lee, Mark, Allie, and Megan were still in Carlene's room.

"I am too tired to walk home," Kathy said.

Hannah rubbed a sore muscle. "Maybe Lee will give us a ride home again."

"I hope so," Roxie said. "I couldn't walk even two steps without falling flat on my face."

Kathy pushed her damp curls back. "We need another day off."

"I wonder when Betina's going to pay us," Chelsea said as she turned an orange around and around in her hand.

Kathy frowned. "I thought this was our good deed."

"So did I," Hannah said.

"No way!" cried Roxie. "You can carry a good deed just so far, you know."

Chelsea jumped up and flipped her red ponytails back. "I turned down other jobs to do this one! I can't afford for this one to be our good deed."

"I think Betina has been planning to pay us," Roxie said. "She read the *King's Kids* ad. She knows doing odd jobs is our business."

Kathy groaned. How could she explain this was to be her good deed to make herself feel better about what she'd said about Megan? "I'll tell Betina not to pay us."

Chelsea and Roxie shook their heads hard. "No way!"

"We should vote," Hannah said. "The majority rules."

"No!" snapped Kathy, jumping up, her cheeks flushed bright red. "We're doing a good deed! That's all there is to it!"

"You're wrong, Kathy," Hannah said gently. "We should vote."

"No!" Kathy shook her banana at Hannah. "I won't vote!"

Hannah's eyes flashed with anger. "I agree with Chelsea and Roxie then. This is not a good deed. We will get paid for it."

Kathy turned away from them, her lips pressed tightly together. She wouldn't agree with them no matter how they voted.

"Let's get out of here," Chelsea snapped. "I don't even want to walk with her!"

"Some people don't know how to be nice," Roxie said.

Kathy's stomach knotted as the girls ran across the yard toward the path through the woods. "Let them go," muttered Kathy. "See if I care."

"Where are they going?" asked Duke as he ran up with Brody beside him.

"Home." Kathy couldn't look at Duke for fear he'd see her anger.

"Why didn't they wait for us?" asked Brody.

"They didn't want to." Kathy wanted to tell Brody to mind his own business, but she was afraid Duke would yell at her.

"Where's Megan?" asked Duke, looking around.

"Upstairs with the others." Kathy looked down at her banana and wondered how she could've thought it looked good. She walked to the fruit basket and dropped it in.

"Go get her," Duke said. "Brody and I have a few more tools to put away, then we'll be ready to leave."

"Race ya," cried Brody.

Duke laughed as he ran after Brody.

Kathy rubbed her aching legs. She was too tired to get Megan, but she slowly walked into the house and up the stairs. The smell of dust was gone, and in its place was the smell of lemon. Sounds of laughing and talking drifted down the hall.

Kathy stopped at Carlene's door. Lee and Betina sat side by side on the floor with Mark, Allie, and Megan sitting in front of them.

Lee looked up with a smile. "Hi, Kathy."

"I came to get Megan. It's time to go home."

"No!" cried Megan, shaking her head hard. "I want to stay with Allie."

"Stay with me!" begged Allie.

Kathy struggled to keep from yelling. "You can't, Megan."

Megan set her jaw stubbornly and didn't move.

"Come on, Megan." Kathy held out her hand.

Megan jumped up and flung her arms around Betina. "Don't let her take me!"

Kathy clenched her fists. She wanted to rip Megan out of Betina's arms and force her out the door.

"You have to go with your sister," Lee said as he gently tugged Megan from Betina. "You can come back again tomorrow."

"Natalie will go with you, honey," Betina said as she stroked Megan's hair.

Kathy's temper shot up, but she wouldn't let the angry words shoot out of her mouth.

With tears in her eyes Megan said, "Bye, Allie. Bye, Mark. We'll be back tomorrow. We have to go, Natalie. I know you don't want to, but you got to."

Kathy caught Megan's hand and pulled her into the hall and down the stairs.

"Don't be mad at me, Kathy."

"Be quiet!"

"You're walking too fast for me and Natalie."

Kathy didn't say a word until they were on the street outside the estate. Then she glared down at Megan. "Natalie is make-believe! Do you hear me?"

"Don't say that!"

"Natalie is only in your imagination. She can't talk to you or play with you! So stop talking *to* her or *about* her!"

Megan jerked away from Kathy and ran down the sidewalk as fast as she could go. Her sandals slapped on the hot sidewalk.

Kathy ran behind Megan, but didn't try to catch her or touch her.

At home Megan ran right to Mom in the living room and clung to her, sobbing as if her heart would break.

As she held Megan to her, Mom looked questioningly at Kathy. "What's wrong? Why is she all sweaty and crying?"

Kathy wiped sweat from her face. Her stomach fluttered. "I told her Natalie wasn't real. I couldn't help it, Mom! She made me so mad!"

"Oh, Kathy," Mom said with great disappointment.

With a strangled sob Kathy ran to her room

and flung herself across her bed. She sobbed against her rag doll. It smelled like fabric softener. After a long time she washed her face in the bathroom. She couldn't look at herself in the mirror.

The Best Friends were angry at her, and so were Mom and Megan. Would she spend her whole life alone?

She groaned heavily. Who could she talk to? Share her secrets with? Who would listen to her tell what she'd done to Megan and not think she was terrible? She missed the Best Friends as if she'd been away from them for weeks instead of an hour.

She ran to the phone in Mom's bedroom and called Chelsea. Her brother Rob answered and said she was gone. Kathy called Roxie. Her sister Lacy answered, as usual, and said Roxie wasn't home. Kathy whimpered as she called Hannah. Her mother said she'd been home, but was gone again.

Sobbing, Kathy ran back to her room. What would she do if she didn't have her friends? Why hadn't she agreed to take pay for working for Betina?

Kathy suddenly felt too closed in to stay inside. She slipped quietly out. From Dad's music room she heard Duke and Brody playing guitars. In the distance a police siren rose and fell. Kathy sat on the picnic table with her feet on the bench, her elbows on her knees, and her chin in her hands. The smell of baking bread drifted across from the back neighbors.

Hearing a sudden sound Kathy looked up, then cried out. Chelsea, Roxie, and Hannah were running toward her.

Kathy leaped to the ground and ran to meet them. She tried to hug them all at the same time as she said over and over, "I'm sorry . . . So sorry! . . . Please forgive me . . . Please."

"We're sorry too," Chelsea said softly.

"Forgive us," Roxie whispered, brushing at her tears.

Kathy hugged them all again. "I vote we get paid for working for Betina," she said brokenly.

"We vote we do it as a good deed," Hannah said.

Kathy pulled away and laughed. They all joined in. Just then Kathy glanced toward the house. Megan stood at the window, and she was looking right at Kathy with wide, sad eyes.

With a moan Kathy turned away, but Megan's sad face stayed in her mind even as she talked with her best friends.

15

A Talk with Dad

Kathy slowly walked to Dad's music room. He had told her to meet him there right after dinner. She'd tried to get out of it, but she couldn't. She knew Mom had told Dad about how upset Megan had been and that it was her fault.

The music room door was open, and Dad sat at the piano playing "Chariots of Fire," a song Kathy had heard Dad play as long as she could remember. It was strange to see Dad play without his ponytail flipping across his back. She liked his short hair, but at times she missed the ponytail. It had always been part of Dad.

He finished the song with great fervor, then spun around on the bench and took Kathy's hand. He tugged her down beside him. "Don't look so frightened. I won't beat you or lock you in a closet."

"I know."

"Forgive me for not having this talk days ago."

Kathy nodded. She wished he'd put it off forever. She smelled his aftershave and a hint of onions on his breath. She thought of all the years she'd sat beside Dad while he played the piano or sat on the floor while he played his guitar or bass or keyboard. The music had become a part of her as much as it had been a part of him.

He tapped the tip of her nose. "Now, tell me what's going on with you."

"I don't know," she whispered.

"Yes, you do. And I know you want to talk about it." Dad rubbed his thumb across her cheek. "I'm here to help."

Kathy bit her lip. "I don't know where to start."

"How about with Megan."

Kathy's eyes flashed. "It's not fair for me to watch her so much! I hate it!"

"I'm sorry, but it has to be that way. We had you watch her to help us all out. We work together as a family to be a family." Dad patted her shoulder. "We couldn't afford to hire a baby-sitter. You've always been a very responsible girl, and we knew we could trust you to take good care of her."

"Why can't Duke help? He doesn't do anything to help the family be a family!"

"He does. But he does other things. He does the yard work, helps with housework, and answers the phone for me."

Kathy twisted the tail of her T-shirt around her finger. "But I could do yard work, and I help with housework. And I'm good at answering the phone."

"And?"

"Why can't we trade off?"

Dad frowned thoughtfully, then nodded. "You have a good point. We'll all talk together about doing that very thing." He ran his long finger over her eyebrows. "I still see a great sadness in your eyes. Suppose you tell me what's causing it."

Kathy's heart jerked. "I can't."

"Sure you can, Kit Kat. I'm your dad, and you can tell me anything."

"Not this," whispered Kathy.

Dad pulled her close and held her tightly. He said against her curls, "Jesus loves you, and I love you. Nothing will ever change that."

She heard the steady beat of his heart and smelled his own special smell. She could close her eyes and have a hundred dads hug her and still pick out her own. She thought of Brody who didn't have a dad to hug him. Brody didn't know his dad's heartbeat or special smell. Tears filled Kathy's eyes. She pulled away from Dad and looked into his dear face. "Dad, please give Brody hugs when he's here."

"I will. But what brought that on?"

She told him, and he kissed her cheeks and said he loved her more than he could say.

"You have a big heart full of love, Kit Kat."

"No, I don't!" she cried, shaking her head hard. In a rush of words she told him how she'd wished Megan was dead like Betina's Carlene. "And I meant it, Dad! I am terrible and not nice at all!"

Dad held Kathy's hands to his heart. "You're not terrible. You're a wonderful girl."

"No, no, I'm not," whispered Kathy.

"Ask Jesus to forgive you for speaking those words, then forgive yourself."

"But I'm too bad!"

"No, Kit Kat. Jesus loves you. He went to the cross, died, and rose again so you wouldn't have to pay for your own sin. He is willing to forgive you. He wants you to forgive yourself."

Kathy remembered all the talks she'd had with her best friends about this very thing. How could she have forgotten it?

"I forgive you," Dad said softly. "Your mom would too, and so would Megan if you asked her. And Jesus is even more willing to forgive than any of us are."

Kathy sniffed back tears and nodded.

Dad pulled her close again and prayed, "Jesus, Kathy is sorry."

"I am, Jesus," whispered Kathy. "Forgive me."

"And, Jesus, help her forgive herself."

"Yes." Kathy instantly knew that Jesus had forgiven her and that she'd forgiven herself. She felt free again.

Dad prayed a while longer while Kathy listened thankfully.

Dad tipped Kathy's head up. "Kit Kat, God has shed His love abroad in your heart by the Holy Ghost. You can love Megan with God's love."

"That's right! I *can* love her with God's love." Kathy smiled.

"I've seen how patient and loving you've been with Megan."

Kathy hung her head. "I was trying to make up for being so bad."

"Now you can be patient and loving because you *are* patient and loving."

Kathy squared her shoulders. "I am!" Silently she thanked God for helping her.

"Let's go talk to Duke and Mom and see about having Duke help with Megan."

"Thanks, Dad."

Hand in hand they walked to the living room. Kathy couldn't wait to see her best friends and tell them all that had happened. They'd cluster around her and shout for joy. That's what best friends were for.

Dad told Mom and Duke about how Kathy felt about baby-sitting Megan, and they worked out a schedule that pleased both Duke and Kathy. Then she walked to Megan's room.

Megan sat up in bed. Her shiny hair hung to the

shoulders of her yellow nightgown. "Kathy, will you read to me?"

"Yes, but first I want to talk to you."

"Okay." Megan moved to give Kathy room to sit beside her.

Kathy brushed soft strands of hair off Megan's flushed cheek. "I'm sorry I said mean things to you about Natalie."

"That's okay. Me and Natalie cried a long time, but we finally quit."

"I'm glad." Kathy pulled Megan onto her lap and held her close. "Megan, you know Natalie is only make-believe, don't you?"

"Yes."

"She's not real."

"I know."

"Good." Kathy nuzzled Megan's neck, and she giggled. "What book do you want me to read?"

Megan squirmed out of Kathy's lap and pulled a book from the shelf. "This one. It's Natalie's favorite. Right, Natalie?"

"Megan!"

She giggled as she crawled back into bed.

Kathy shook her head and laughed, then opened the book. She couldn't remember a time when she was ever happier than right now.